THE OBNOXIOUS JERKS

Ippolito gave me this horrible look. Then he shook his head, gathered himself together, and stepped bravely onto the porch. "Come on. The coast is clear."

"I'm just checking to make sure I've got my keys."

"Stalling," he said. "You're just stalling. Hurry it up! I see some kids way up the street."

"I'm not stalling. There aren't any pockets in this skirt. Where'd you put *your* keys?"

"In my purse, stupid," he joked, then stopped short. "Oh, man!"

I knew what he was thinking before he even said it. "Forget 'em, right?"

Ippolito looked sheepish. "Oh, well. We keep a spare outside."

"What about your wallet?"

"That I've got!" he said confidently. Suddenly he looked slightly sick. "I think." He took his bookpack off his shoulders and looked in the outer pocket. Then he looked in the book compartment. "My dear," he said. "I'm sure you won't mind lending me the wherewithal for lunch."

"Delighted. Now, after you."

"No, my dear, I insist. After you."

We probably would've stood there all day, ex... really were getting cl... r courage and hit th... going to be the b... all time, or the absolute, total, and co... worst. Assuming we lived through it.

The Obnoxious Jerks

Stephen Manes

BANTAM BOOKS
NEW YORK · TORONTO · LONDON · SYDNEY · AUCKLAND

For Rog, Rich, and Dave
(who were)
and Steve and Deanna
(who should have been)

RL5, ages 12 and up

THE OBNOXIOUS JERKS

A Bantam Book
Bantam hardcover edition / August 1988
Bantam paperback edition / February 1990

*The Starfire logo is a registered trademark of Bantam Books,
a division of Bantam Doubleday Dell Publishing Group, Inc.
Registered in U.S. Patent and Trademark Office and elsewhere.*

LIBRARY OF CONGRESS
Library of Congress Cataloging-in-Publication Data

Manes, Stephen, 1949–
 The obnoxious jerks / Stephen Manes.
  p.   cm.
 Summary: High school sophomore Frank Wess relates his experiences
as a member of the Obnoxious Jerks, an elite body dedicated to
exposing both official and unofficial stupidity.
 ISBN 0-553-28114-3 (U.S.)
 [1. Clubs—Fiction. 2. High schools—Fiction. 3. Schools—
Fiction. 4. Humorous stories.] I. Title.
PZ7.M31264Ob   1988
[Fic]—dc19   88-10498
                                                  CIP
                                                  AC

Published simultaneously in the United States and Canada

*Bantam Books are published by Bantam Books, a division of Bantam
Doubleday Dell Publishing Group, Inc. Its trademark, consisting of the
words "Bantam Books" and the portrayal of a rooster, is Registered in
U.S. Patent and Trademark Office and in other countries. Marca
Registrada. Bantam Books, 666 Fifth Avenue, New York, New York 10103.*

PRINTED IN THE UNITED STATES OF AMERICA

OPM   0 9 8 7 6 5 4 3 2

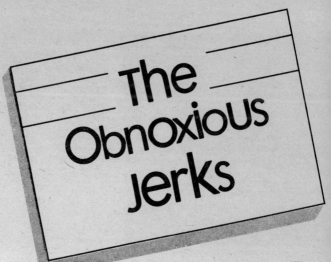

The Obnoxious Jerks

1

It sounded great in theory. But now it wasn't theory anymore. It was reality. And in reality it felt like the stupidest thing I had ever done in my entire life.

I stood in front of the mirror and adjusted my skirt. Stupid, all right. I looked amazingly stupid. Incredibly stupid. From every angle.

I tried to pull the skirt down a little. Even stupider. I yanked it up some. Worse. I wondered if maybe it would look less stupid if I changed my shirt. Or my socks. Or my shoes. Or my knees. Or something. Anything!

I sat down on my bed and took off my shoes. I wondered if my underwear showed when I sat down. I couldn't quite get the right angle to check it in the mirror.

But I was a first-timer. A total novice. I didn't have any idea how you were supposed to handle these things. What do guys know about wearing skirts, anyhow?

The worst part of it all was that it was my own

fault. The whole thing was actually my idea. Served me right for opening my big mouth. And for doing a favor for this girl just because she actually seemed kind of interesting.

I looked in the mirror again. The skirt looked stupider than ever. Well, it was my own damned fault. I probably should have guessed something like this was bound to happen when I became an Obnoxious Jerk.

2

It all began months before on a day I was not likely to forget. "In less than fifteen minutes, you, Frank Wess, will officially be an Obnoxious Jerk," Joe Ippolito told me that fateful gray November afternoon at Harry Schwarzkopf's house.

"It's a genuine honor," I replied almost sincerely.

"And a big responsibility, son," Ippolito said in a mock-fatherly tone, putting an arm around my shoulders. "I just hope you can handle it."

"The initiation ceremony will touch you beyond belief," Wilver Sims stated solemnly. "It is a memory you will cherish the rest of your life."

"It's absolutely unique," agreed Mike "Planet" Daley. "When you become one of us, you will feel a rush of power not lightly given to mortal men."

"I can hardly wait," I said snidely. Ippolito had already warned me these guys would lay the sarcasm on thick.

"Have some Jalapeño Flavor Chipiritos!" said Aristides "Wrist" Demetrios, extending a double handful out to me. "They build the mind and character of the true Obnoxious Jerk."

I took a few out of his hands and stuffed them into my mouth.

"Don't skimp," Schwarzkopf insisted, pointing to the big bowls of chips all around his rec room. "Jalapeño Flavor Chipiritos are the Official Tortilla Chip of the Obnoxious Jerks. And don't forget Doola Cola, either."

"It's the Official Cola Beverage of the Obnoxious Jerks," Perry Wu pointed out.

"The nectar of the Jerk," I joked.

Three or four guys gave me horrified stares. "Didn't anybody tell you?" demanded Wilver Sims.

"Didn't anybody tell me what?" I replied.

"There are jerks, and there are Obnoxious Jerks," said Roberto Garcia. "Jerks are everybody else. *We* are *Obnoxious* Jerks. Don't ever get the two confused."

"Or refer to us as O.J.'s," added Daley. "Glasses of orange juice, a certain great football player, and an old soul music group are O.J.'s. We are Obnoxious Jerks."

"It's our one and only sacred rule," said Dennis "The Schneid" Schneider. "Violations are punishable by a fine of twenty-seven cents, plus tax. Fortunately you are not an official member yet."

"Sorry," I said. "I was a jerk. Now I know better."

As I dug into one of the chip bowls, Ippolito stood up and announced, "All rise for our national anthem."

Except Ippolito didn't stand up. Neither did anybody else except Demetrios and Daley. I looked at Ippolito for a hint. He just shrugged, so I didn't bother to get up.

"Ta-da!" Ippolito said with a kind of war whoop. "Take it away, Leon, take it away!"

There wasn't anybody named Leon in the room. But Daley and Demetrios put their arms around each other's

4

shoulders and harmonized. As a country music nut, I recognized the tune—Bob Wills's Texas Playboys' theme—but the last two lines were new to me:

> If you're traveling near or far
> And you want to know who we are
> We're the Obnoxious Jerks
> And you can stick it in your ear!

"The occasional meeting of the Obnoxious Jerks is hereby called to order," said Ippolito, pounding an empty Doola Cola can on the table.

"Order!" mumbled Roberto Garcia.

"Two all-beef patties, secret sauce, lettuce, cheese, pickles, onions, and vomit on a sesame-seed bun," Schwarzkopf called out. "To go."

"Schwarzkopf means 'blackhead' in German," Demetrios whispered to me so loud that everybody else could hear. I knew a little German; Demetrios was actually right.

"Demetrios means 'oozing, festering boil' in any language," Schwarzkopf whispered back. Somehow I doubted that.

"Did I call this meeting to order or what?" Ippolito asked.

"Order!" Garcia repeated. "We're trying to get things rolling. A little order, please, gentlemen."

"One thirtieth of an all-beef patty, secret sauce—"

"Schwarzkopf, will you please shut up?" The Schneid requested.

Schwarzkopf grinned. "He did say a *little* order, and one thirtieth of an all-beef patty is just a *tiny*, minute, infinitesimal—"

"Schwarzkopf, if you don't shut up, we're going to have the sergeant at arms eject you," Ippolito said.

"We don't have a sergeant at arms. We don't even have a sergeant at legs," Schwarzkopf replied.

5

"*I'll* eject you if you don't shut up," said Demetrios.

"Yeah? You and who else?"

"Me!" cried the rest of the room.

"Guess maybe I reckon I'll hush my mouth, then, pardners," Schwarzkopf said. "My lips are sealed." He moved his hand across them like a zipper.

"All right," said Ippolito. "I guess I have to ask if there's any old business. Is there?"

"Wait a minute. You forgot to read the minutes of the last meeting," said Demetrios.

"Oh, yeah. Who was the secretary for the last meeting?" Ippolito asked.

Wilver Sims raised his hand. "Yo."

"Okay," said Ippolito. "Read the minutes."

"There are no minutes," said Sims. "We never take minutes."

"May I have a motion to waive the reading of the minutes?" said Ippolito.

"So moved," said Schwarzkopf.

"Seconded," said Demetrios.

"All in favor?"

There was a loud chorus of "Aye" with a couple of "yi-yi"'s thrown in.

"All opposed?"

Schwarzkopf neighed like a horse.

"Motion carried. May we have the report of the treasurer?"

Demetrios stood up. "At the beginning of the last meeting our treasury stood at precisely no dollars, no cents, and four bags of Chipirito Jalapeño Flavor Tortilla Chips. After collecting dues at the end of the last meeting, we infinitely improved our cash assets. We now have precisely no dollars and four cents. Plus four bags of Chipirito Jalapeño Flavor Chips. Minus whatever anybody's eaten since the beginning of the meeting."

"I move we count the chips," Schwarzkopf said. "Just to make sure there's been no embezzlement."

"Motion denied," said Ippolito. "And thank you, official temporary treasurer. Any old business?"

"Is the attire committee new business or old business?" Wu asked.

"How much tread is left?" said Schwarzkopf.

Wu fell for it. "Huh?"

"On the tire committee," Schwarzkopf replied. Nobody even bothered to groan.

"I deem it old business," said Ippolito. "Where's the chair of the attire committee?"

Wilver Sims stood up, picked up the chair he was sitting on, and held it aloft with one hand. "Yo."

"The chair hereby recognizes the chair of the attire committee," said Ippolito.

"He ought to recognize it, all right," said Roberto Garcia. "It looks just like his sister."

Everybody laughed and hooted. "Order!" Ippolito shouted, banging the Doola Cola can on the table. "Order! Actually, that chair looks *better* than my sister."

"Yo," said Sims, sitting down. "You want the report from the attire committee or not?"

"Proceed," said Ippolito.

Wilver Sims stood up. "Report from the attire committee: We're working on it." Sims sat down again.

"Wait a minute," Ippolito replied. "That's it?"

Wilver Sims stood up. "That's it." He sat down again.

"Hold the phone!" shouted Wrist Demetrios.

Schwarzkopf picked up a phone from the table beside him. "Got it!"

"Seriously," Demetrios said. "We were supposed to have those shirts by now."

Wilver Sims stood up again. "We're working on it." He sat down.

"Wait a second!" Demetrios said. "Who else is on the committee?"

Perry Wu and Planet Daley lazily raised their hands.

"Well, what's the story?" Demetrios demanded.

"Once upon a time we tried to get some shirts," said Daley.

"It's not as easy as it looks," said Perry Wu.

Wilver Sims stood up again. "We're working on it." He sat down.

"What's not easy about it?" Garcia inquired. "You can get a shirt in five minutes down at the mall! Complete with customized lettering. Anything you want."

"Right," said Wu. "But who wants some dumb shirt you can buy down at the stupid old mall?"

"We are talking about class here," said Daley. "We are not talking about just any old dumb club."

"We are talking about the particular dumb club known as the Obnoxious Jerks," Schwarzkopf snorted.

"Right with bells on," Daley agreed. "Now I ask you: Do the Obnoxious Jerks deserve some lame shirt anybody could buy down at the mall—or do they deserve the finest shirts the apparel world has to offer?"

"Some lame shirt, of course," said The Schneid.

Perry Wu frowned. "Give us a week. We've got a lead on some of the finest shirts in America. We're trying to get a good price."

Wilver Sims stood up.

"We know, we know," Ippolito said before Sims could open his mouth.

Wilver Sims sat down again.

"More old business?" Ippolito asked. Nobody said anything. "New business?"

Schwarzkopf raised his hand. "I wish to nominate a list of fine items for consideration as official products of the Obnoxious Jerks."

"Oh, no," Demetrios muttered. "Not again."

"Jalapeño Flavor Chipiritos and Doola Cola are only the beginning," said Schwarzkopf. "I am now proposing the Official Lubricant: Mr. Slippy. The Official Ice Cream Flavor: Nuts to You. The Official Snack Cake: Devil Dogs. The Official Dip: Jumpin' Bean. The Official—"

"How long is this list?" Demetrios demanded.

"You'll find out when I get to the end," Schwarzkopf said. "Where was I? Oh, yeah, the Official Paper Towel: Brawny. The Official—"

"Come on, Harry," Garcia interrupted. "Give us a break."

Schwarzkopf scowled. "I believe I have the floor. The Official—"

Ippolito pounded his Doola Cola can on the table. "Harry, there's a limit. We are about to invoke cloture here."

"Cloture? Cloture?" Schwarzkopf said indignantly.

"You had Nilon for social studies, so you know darn well what it means," Daley said. "The limitation of speech."

"But you can't do it while I have the floor," Schwarzkopf claimed.

"Who said?" demanded Wilver Sims.

"It's a well-known fact," Schwarzkopf replied. "I dare you."

"We are about to take a vote for cloture," said Joe Ippolito. "All those in favor . . ."

A flood of *aye*'s drowned out Schwarzkopf's "I protest!"

"All those opposed?"

"Railroaded!" said Schwarzkopf. "I've been railroaded!"

"Good. You need training, son. Any more new business?"

"Wait a minute!" Schwarzkopf protested. "Can't we even vote on the ones I proposed already?"

"He's got a point," said Perry Wu.

"Yeah, and we know where," said Planet Daley.

"What about discussion?" said Ippolito. "There might be opposition."

"Right," said Demetrios. "None of those Devil Dogs for me. I'm a Hostess Snowball man myself."

"You look more like a Twinkie," said Daley.

Garcia spoke up. "If you ask me—"

"And we didn't," Schwarzkopf interrupted.

Garcia ignored him. "—a lot of these things are too corporate. I thought we decided to avoid big-name products in favor of the little guys."

"Hear, hear," said Demetrios.

"All right, all right," said Schwarzkopf, consulting his list. "Can we at least agree on the official lubricant, ice cream flavor, dip, and paper towel?"

"We can agree on the official dip, all right," said Roberto Garcia. "You."

"I decline the nomination," said Schwarzkopf, "in favor of Mr. Bean."

"I'll go along with the dip and the ice cream flavor. The rest I'll fight on general principle," Garcia said.

"All right, all right," said Ippolito. "Any further discussion?"

Meaningless mumbles rippled through the room.

"All in favor of the proposed dip and ice cream flavor, please signify by clucking like a chicken."

The room sounded like a riot in a barnyard.

"All opposed, stand up and do a silly dance."

Nobody did, but Schwarzkopf stood up and bowed. Demetrios and Daley threw Jalapeño Flavor Chipiritos at him and told him to sit down.

"There is one more piece of new business," Ippolito said. "We have a new member to induct. I'm referring to Frank Wess over there."

I raised my hand slightly and said "Present."

"Do I hear a motion to include Frank Wess as a member of the Obnoxious Jerks?"

"Why not?" said Mike Daley.

"Do I hear a second?"

"Second!" Perry Wu mumbled.

"Moved and seconded," said Garcia. "All in favor, please bellow like a sick cow."

General racket.

"All opposed, stand on your head and lick the soles of your shoes."

Nobody did.

"I now pronounce you, Frank Wess, a full-fledged one-hundred-percent Obnoxious Jerk!" said Joe Ippolito. "Stand by for the Obnoxious Jerk salute!"

Everybody but me stuffed his hands and mouth with Jalapeño Flavor Chipiritos and crunched as loud as he could. On cue from Ippolito, everybody shouted "Caramba!" Chipiritos went flying everywhere.

For a moment I almost felt a rush of power not lightly given to mortal men. "I will never forget this touching ceremony as long as I live," I said.

And then a tear ran down my cheek. Those Jalapeño Flavor Chipirito crumbs can really sting your eyes.

3

It really was a momentous day for me. About an hour after I became an official Obnoxious Jerk and finished picking Jalapeño Flavor Chipiritos out of my sweater, I also got a new official nickname: "Back," for "Back Wess," pronounced as closely as possible to "backwards." Ippolito kept chuckling about it as we walked home afterward.

"I still don't understand how the whole thing happened," I said. "It sure wasn't intentional or anything."

"Sure was hilarious, though," Ippolito said, running a mental replay.

I made a face. I had won the nickname for my dazzling performance in the touch football game after the meeting—but not because I was any good at full, half, quarter, running, or any other backfield position. Nope. What turned me into "Back" Wess was a truly amazing fourth-down punt. Somehow—talk about talent! —I'd managed to kick the ball over my head and behind me and the line of scrimmage and then fall down on my rear end. The other side retrieved the ball about two steps away from the goal line and ran it over for the winning score in about two seconds.

"God, was that embarrassing," I said. "I still can't believe it."

"Forget it," Ippolito told me. "Obnoxious Jerks don't believe winning isn't everything. Especially when you lose. You had fun, didn't you?"

"Yeah," I admitted, "till I screwed up that punt."

"Hey, it wasn't all that much worse than what the rest of us did. I mean, it was worse, yeah, but not all that much worse. Who'd you see who looked any good out there?"

"Sims looked pretty good," I said.

"Sims always looks pretty good when he plays in our games, 'cause he's got at least a couple of inches and forty pounds on the rest of us. In a real game? Forget it! They kicked him out of tryouts two years running. Too slow."

I couldn't believe it. Sims was a big black guy, but he was the gentle, quiet type, with an almost sneaky sense of humor. "Sims actually went out for the team?"

"Don't hold it against him. We all make mistakes. If somebody thinks what he really wants to do with his life is get his brains scrambled in a scrimmage, that's his business. Actually, I think it was more his dad's business—his father was some kind of star in college or something. Anyway, Sims probably won't go out for football again. He's too into his biology stuff. He's working on some sort of project I don't understand three words of. Heavy duty."

I laughed. "Well, at least he didn't look one-hundred-percent stupid out there."

"Hey, you're going to look stupid sooner or later. May as well be sooner. Obnoxious Jerks expect that. So don't worry about it. Be proud to be a part of our organization's glorious history. Hey, we're legends in our own minds."

Actually, the Obnoxious Jerks were slightly more famous than that. Back when he'd asked me to join up, Ippolito had filled me in on the glorious past of the organization. It had started in ninth grade. Ippolito and Schwarzkopf and Daley—and Perry Wu when he got over his shyness enough for them to realize he was basically okay—started hanging out together once a week or so after school. They called themselves the After-School Suet and Slime Society, because they were all really big on horror movies at the time. Wu was into them so much he put together some kind of electronic gadget that would cause superrealistic "blood" explosions just like in the movies, but he could never get human volunteers, because his test dummies kept going up in flames.

When ASSASS finally added more members, everybody agreed they needed a classier name to impress girls. They finally decided on the Playboys of the Western Movies. According to Ippolito, the only girl it ever impressed was Planet Daley's six-year-old sister.

Anyway, one day in fifth-period social studies, Old Man Nilon was going on and on about the electoral college, and Daley challenged him on some little point about the way it used to work in the old days. Nilon insisted he was all wrong and said something snotty like "The day I take history lessons from a freshman is the day I'll pack it in."

But Daley had been a history buff since he read *Johnny Tremain* in third grade, and he was sure he knew what he was talking about. So Ippolito and Sims and Demetrios lent him a hand. Right in the middle of one particularly boring class, while Nilon was droning on about something or other, they all got up from their seats, shouted, "Pack it in!" and dumped a pile of paper on Nilon's desk—evidence that proved Daley had been absolutely right.

They kept chanting "Admit he's right or pack it in!" But Nilon didn't do either one. He was so angry at being embarrassed in front of the class that he sent the four troublemakers to the principal's office. As he was writing out their hall pass, he muttered loud enough so that the whole class could hear, "You know, guys, you really are obnoxious jerks." That afternoon, by unanimous vote, the Playboys of the Western Movies officially became the Obnoxious Jerks.

"You're either Obnoxious Jerk material or you're not," Ippolito had said when he invited me to join. "I mean, you, now. You are definitely Obnoxious Jerk material."

I didn't take that as an insult. Somehow you knew where you fit into the scheme of things at Ullman Griswold Memorial High—UGMH on the official insignia, just plain UGH to most of us. There was the heavy-metal crowd, there was the drug crowd, there was the dope crowd—not drugs, just terminal stupidity—there was the jock crowd, there was the social-climber Student-Council suck-up-to-the-teachers crowd, and there were the poor humorless nerds. If you didn't qualify for any of those cliques (the brain-dead, Schwarzkopf called them all), you had to be a total misfit—which made you perfect Obnoxious Jerk material.

I knew I was a misfit pretty soon after I transferred to UGH for my sophomore year. My dad and mom are both software engineers with the same company, and they keep getting promoted and having to move around, so I've never lived in the same house or apartment building or even the same town three years in a row. And when we moved to Froston from Georgia, I was positive I was going to hate it. For one thing, the weather stank. It rained all the time. When it didn't rain, it was cloudy.

15

And rumor had it winters were about as cold as they come.

Even though it was near a pretty big city, it was real suburban, which meant unless you had a car—and forget it, I still had nearly a year to go till I could get my learner's permit—there wasn't a whole hell of a lot to do, unless you wanted to go up to the college and get hassled by the college kids. The big deals in town were football in the fall and basketball in the winter and rock music all year long. We moved there in August, and as far as I could tell, there wasn't anybody around who was anything like the weird, smart friends I had back in Georgia.

Sometimes moving is okay, and sometimes it isn't. I remembered all the times in the past I'd had to start fresh at a new school, but it never seemed to get any easier. When classes started, I knew pretty quickly I wasn't going to fit in. Some of the kids kissed up to the teachers so much it was sickening. Some of the kids were so stupid they could barely walk down the hall and chew gum at the same time. And nobody went out of the way to make friends with a new kid who was too small for football, too short for basketball, and couldn't give less of a damn about acid rock or doing drugs.

Except the Obnoxious Jerks. The way I hooked up with them was weird. There was some substitute teacher in Adamec's math class, a woman so dull she would have found a way to make things boring even if she'd stood up on her desk and taken all her clothes off. So I kind of absentmindedly began to while away the time by playing music on my teeth. It was a skill I'd developed to keep from falling asleep in fourth-grade health class in Mississippi, where I had a real stupefying teacher named Miss Jarney. The first tune I ever learned was "Yankee Doodle"; by the time I got to Froston, I had a pretty decent repertoire, including everything from classical symphonies to classic rock.

Anyhow, this particular dull day with the sub up front in Adamec's class, this guy in front of me who had never said three words to me in the first month or so of school suddenly leaned back and asked me in a whisper if I'd ever heard Bill Monroe's version of the tune I was playing—"Jerusalem Ridge." The guy in front of me was Joe Ippolito, and he turned out to be the only other kid I'd ever met anywhere who knew anything at all about bluegrass. He played mandolin, and I played banjo, and neither one of us was very good, and we got to be friends. I joined up with him and his gang for lunch, and a week later I was asked to come to the meeting.

"We had our eye on you as Obnoxious Jerk material from the beginning," Ippolito said as we headed home. "We liked the way you answered in class and stuff like that. You can just kind of tell. But for a while there we thought you were a real loner—always eating alone in the cafeteria, that kind of thing. Basically we wanted to make sure you weren't a wimp."

"Thanks for the support," I said.

"Well, we can't be too careful. Once you're in, you're in. Membership in the Obnoxious Jerks is for life. There's no way you can get kicked out."

"Or punted out?" I joked.

"Will you give that a rest? You want to hang out with people who worry about backward punts, hang out with the Lords. Or the Viscounts."

The Viscounts were the club for the social-climbing bootlicker crowd. The Lords were the jocks.

"Right," I said sarcastically. "And go through that famous Hell Night George Alton keeps bragging about."

"I used to have homeroom with that pond scum. He's in your homeroom now, right?"

I nodded. "Yeah. Lucky me. All you ever hear him talk about is how tough he is because he went through Hell Night. Every time I hear him yakking away about how tough Hell Night was and how he was the only sophomore who made it through, I know my idea of hell is having to listen to him."

"Why don't you tell him that?" Ippolito joked.

"I kind of like my body to be free of bruises and blemishes," I said. Alton was the kind of cheap bully who liked picking fights with people smaller than he was, which was just about everybody in our class.

"Hey, everybody knows Alton's scum," Ippolito said.

"Everybody but the Lords. And Coach Arborio. And the idiots who elected him to Student Council."

"Takes scum to know scum. Did I ever tell you about the name we nearly voted in back before we became the Obnoxious Jerks?"

I shook my head.

"We thought it would be kind of neat to poke fun at clubs that were named after hereditary feudal titles. You know: Lords, Viscounts. So Daley came up with a great name for the group."

"Don't keep me in suspense or anything."

"Serf City, U.S.A."

I cracked up. "Why didn't you go with it?"

"We had a big debate. When it was all over, we decided the only kids in the school who'd get it would be us. The rest probably would think we misspelled 'surf.' That is, the ones who knew how to spell."

4

It's not exactly clear how the human brain functions—particularly mine. But as I stood there in my skirt months after I became an Obnoxious Jerk, I remembered that in a major way my brilliant skirt-wearing career dated back to my second Obnoxious Jerks meeting, which was held at Demetrios's house with Roberto Garcia as chairman of the week. One special feature of this meeting was the brand-new Official Dip that accompanied our usual bowlfuls of the Official Chip. The Schneid said the combination of Jumpin' Bean and Chipiritos was the kind of thing they warned you about in health class. Planet Daley said it had to be called Jumpin' Bean because it kept you hopping.

But the important thing was the report from the attire committee. "Report from the attire committee," said Wilver Sims. "We've been working on it." He sat down.

"Aw, come on," Schwarzkopf whined. "This has gone

on long enough. We need those shirts. We have to have them for this jerk-out."

Sims stood up again. "We've been working on it." He sat back down.

"For once in his demented life, Schwarzkopf is right," said The Schneid. "We can't wait much longer. It's insane."

"Ta-da!" said Planet Daley, reaching into a big shopping bag. Suddenly he and Wu began flinging big shirts around the room. Garcia pounded his can of Doola Cola on the table and called for order, but a shirt landed on his head and ended that idea.

In the general pandemonium, one of the shirts landed on me. I held it out to take a look. For one thing, it was huge—about seven sizes too big for anybody under three hundred pounds. Second, it was a kind of sickening purplish color. Third, there was a downright puky orange letter on the back. Or maybe it was a number: a big O.

I looked around. The other T-shirts were all huge, but they were all different colors—truly disgusting ones. They also had lettering on the back, but the letters were all different. Some of the shirts had only one letter; some had two.

"These are the official shirts?" I asked Ippolito.

He held one up to his chest and beamed. "Aren't they great?"

I shrugged. "They're not all the same. Not even close."

"That's the point," Perry Wu said, shaking his head.

"I don't get it," I said.

"Did you ever read the UGH dress code?" Wu asked.

I nodded. The dress code was prominently featured in the *Ullman Griswold Memorial High School Student Handbook*. Enforcing it seemed to be the one thing the administration was proudest of.

"Well?" Wu said.

"Well, what?" I replied wittily.

"Think about it. What's not allowed?" Wu said.

I thought about it.

"Come on, Back," Ippolito taunted, waving his huge bright red shirt in front of him like a bullfighter. "You mean you didn't memorize the famous dress code?"

"Hold on. Let me get it," I said, thinking out loud. "No shirts without collars. No cutoffs or shorts. No sweatshirts. Nothing see-through, unfortunately. Jeans must not be blue." I stopped to think some more.

"What else?" Wu demanded.

"Oh, yeah. Socks. You have to wear socks."

"Or stockings. Or panty hose," Perry Wu said. Somebody tossed a T-shirt at him. "What else?" Wu prodded.

I threw my hands in the air. "I give up."

Wu shook his finger at me. "No uniforms or insignia of any social group or organization except school sports teams."

"So?" I asked.

"So this is a uniform that's not a uniform. It's insignia without insignia. Get it?"

"No," I said.

He grabbed Schwarzkopf's T-shirt and held his own out next to it so I could read the backs. They spelled OU on the top and E on the bottom. He stared at me. "Get it?"

I didn't.

"If you put them in the right order, they spell out OBNOXIOUS on top and JERKS on the bottom."

I slapped my forehead. Was I thick or what?

"So how can anybody say we're violating the dress code?" said Wu.

"They can't, that's how," said Sims. "It's not a uniform, because there's nothing uniform about it. Every shirt is totally different."

"Except in size," Wu said. "We got all the same size."

"We wanted to be sure to observe the dress code business about shirts having to be tucked in," Sims said. "We thought these would look really dumb stuffed under your belt."

Demetrios was staring at his shirt as though it were the most beautiful thing he had ever seen. "These really are great," he said. "Nice job, guys."

"In case you're interested, they come from the only big-and-tall-men's bowling supply store in the country," said Daley.

"Pretty neat, huh?" said Sims.

I nodded. "I can't believe it took me so long to get it."

"It's okay," said Daley sarcastically. "When you've been one of us long enough, you'll build a reserve of mental power not lightly given to mortal men."

Garcia pounded on the table with his Doola Cola can. "Could we get this meeting going again?"

"I move we thank the attire committee for a job well done, which is rare around here," said The Schneid.

"Second," half of us shouted.

"All in favor, signify by raising your middle finger high in the air," said Garcia.

Many middle fingers, many loud huzzahs.

"All opposed, signify by spreading Jumpin' Bean dip in your navel and dipping it out with a Chipirito."

Schwarzkopf lifted his sweater to reveal his belly button, but The Schneid grabbed the dip away before he could gross us out.

"Any more new business?" Garcia demanded.

Schwarzkopf stood up. "I have more nominees for official products of the Obnoxious Jerks."

Everybody groaned, including me. I had a vote now too.

"Come on, Harry. Give us a break. Just once?" Garcia begged.

Wilver Sims stood up. "We've got a whole strategy session to get through here, not to mention some heavy-duty football. As chairman of the attire committee, I urge you not to force us to invoke cloture." He subtly pounded his left fist into his right hand.

"Oh, all right," said Schwarzkopf, sitting down. "But I've got some real great ones here. You have to admit the bean dip was a winner."

"We'll send you a thank-you note from the bathroom," said The Schneid. "We'll probably all be there for the next three days."

"Too true," said Planet Daley. "But by the time we come out on Monday morning, we will be cleansed, purified, and ready to do battle with the forces of evil—otherwise known as the administration of Ullman Griswold Memorial Prison. This is going to be our best jerk-out ever."

5

Since I came in late, the great shirt caper was my first jerk-out ever. Jerk-outs were a tradition of the Obnoxious Jerks that went all the way back to the start of the school year. For a while the members thought they should be called jerk-offs, but somebody pointed out that would be playing into the enemy's hands, since that's what the administration would call them—though not to our faces, of course.

The official idea behind the jerk-out was to challenge stupidity. The first one I'd ever heard about was the week all the members of The Obnoxious Jerks came to school wearing designer jeans—not blue ones, of course—with the names and insignia deliberately crossed out with marking pen. It was kind of a quiet protest against all the brain-dead kids who thought they were hot stuff because of the clothes they wore. Unfortunately it turned out a lot like the Serf City, U.S.A. idea: The brain-dead kids didn't get it. They thought the

Obnoxious Jerks must have bought defective clothes at a factory outlet or something.

The other big jerk-out was a kind of protest about the rule that only administration-approved literature could be distributed in the school. This meant that the only things anybody could hand out were our lame official paper, *The Griswold Gazette,* and these moronic official letters from the school administration. Some of the Obnoxious Jerks wanted to start a magazine of satire poking fun at school stupidity, but nobody wanted to waste time doing it if you couldn't hand it out. It would have been cool if they could have found some teacher to serve as faculty adviser, but when they tried, they discovered even the hipper teachers didn't want the hassle of being hooked up with a publication that might hint the administration was less than a model of human perfection.

It was hopeless, but they decided to take one stab at it anyway. With the help of The Schneid's computer and his father's Xerox machine, the Obnoxious Jerks produced a letter that looked exactly like an official school document, right down to the letterhead and Principal Helena Rojewski's signature. The only difference was that all it said was "Blah, blah, blah" all the way down the page. The brain-dead didn't get the joke, the rule didn't change, and the perpetrators served a week of detention. But as Ippolito says, "Improving the world is a slow process."

So on Monday morning as I tucked my enormous billowy Obnoxious Jerks shirt into my pants, I felt a little bit edgy about the jerk-out. I was still pretty new in the school. The last thing I needed was to make trouble for myself with the administration. From what I'd heard, they could make trouble for you later on when you went to them for your college recommendations.

But on the other hand I was an Obnoxious Jerk and proud of it. So on that cold Monday morning I had my giant orange-lettered lavender bowling shirt on as I waited outside school for the rest of the Obnoxious Jerks to arrive. The wind was fierce; we all wore jackets for warmth and camouflage. Finally everybody was there but Demetrios.

"We'll give him a couple minutes more," said The Schneid, rubbing his hands together to keep warm. "If he doesn't show up, we'll have to come up with an alternate plan."

Demetrios showed up, all right. But when he met us at the door, he looked kind of sheepish. His jacket was open and he was wearing a sweater underneath it, which wasn't a bad idea on a day like this. But where was his shirt?

"Didn't you forget something?" Planet Daley asked him as he came up to us.

Demetrios shook his head.

"Where's your shirt?" Perry Wu demanded.

"I don't want to get in trouble. My dad will give me too much hassle if I have to do detention again."

"Hey, you were the one who said this was going to be great," Ippolito reminded him.

"Yeah, but if I get detention or suspension my dad will kill me, that's all."

"Come on," said Sims. "Look at all the work the committee put into this."

"I'm sorry," Demetrios said, and he really did sound that way. "That's it. That's how it has to be."

Garcia started booing him, the way you boo an umpire. "Hey, cut that out," said Ippolito.

"Why should I?" Garcia said. "He's spoiling everything."

"Right," said Ippolito. "But that's his business."

"Hey, it's our business too," said Daley.

"Article One of the Obnoxious Jerks' Philosophy,"

Ippolito reminded us. "Do not conform to any organization or rule, including this one."

Everybody kind of stammered a little. Demetrios looked grateful. "It does make it kind of tough, Wrist," Ippolito pointed out. "You've got the middle shirt."

"So he'll trade with whoever's got the end shirt— the one with just the S on top," said Perry Wu. "You —Roberto."

"Wait a minute," said Sims. "That's no good. Then it ends up saying OBNOXIOU JERKS."

"It's better than nothing," Garcia said.

"It's terminally dumb," said Schwarzkopf.

"It's dumb, all right," Ippolito said. "But not dumb enough. That's the problem."

"Hey, let's just go without Wrist. Leave out the middle shirt," said The Schneid.

"OBNOIOUS JEKS," Schwarzkopf said aloud. "That has a nice ring to it."

"OBNOIOUS JEKS," said Garcia. "Yeah. Let's do it."

"Sure you won't come with us?" Sims asked Demetrios.

"Like to," Wrist said. "Can't."

"Not even for moral support?" Wu asked.

Demetrios shook his head kind of sadly. "I'll see you guys at lunch, okay? Let me know how it turns out." He trudged inside.

"Don't count on it," Schwarzkopf called after him. "If you're right, we'll be suspended by then."

"Give him a break," said Daley. "If the guy's got problems at home, the guy's got problems at home. No sense making them worse."

"So are we ready?" Wu asked.

"Like Freddy," said The Schneid.

"Ready, willing, and able," said Garcia.

"Let's do it," said Wilver Sims.

We all let up a little cheer of "All right!" and "Go

27

for it!" and such. Then we went inside and turned the corner toward the principal's offices. We all took off our jackets and kind of milled around. We were ready to jump into the positions we needed to spell out OBNOX- IOUS JERKS—sorry, OBNOIOUS JEKS—but we decided to keep the letters mixed up until the very last moment. Of course, the crazy-colored bowling shirts weren't exactly what you'd wear if you didn't want to attract attention.

"Oh, God," said George Alton as he passed by. "You pitiful turds."

"You're where they come from," said Perry Wu, moving directly behind Sims.

Mighty Lord Alton, the only sophomore to survive Hell Night, stopped dead in his tracks. "Who said that?"

"We all did," said Wilver Sims, stepping forward.

"Look at those miserable shirts," Alton sneered. "You wiseasses are gonna get yours one of these days."

"If you're the one who's planning to do it, we'll have a long wait," Sims said.

"Yeah, why don't you just go on to class like a good boy?" Schwarzkopf said. "You certainly could use some book-learning."

"I'm telling you ..." Alton warned, shaking his finger at us, but then Sims took a step toward him. Alton backed away and continued down the hall, pointing a different finger at us.

"Hey! Here he comes! Crawley!" said Wu.

"Assume the positions!" said Garcia.

Of course, Schwarzkopf had to go to the wrong spot in the line just to gag things up and spell OBOIONUS EKSJ. But we shoved him around to the right place in time to get it right—that is, if you called OBNOIOUS JEKS right. So we were all set as "Creepy" Crawley, the vice-principal, headed straight toward us. Crawley was the guy who did most of the disciplinary work when disciplinary work had to be done. I hadn't met up with him personally myself, but he always looked as though he had just smelled something awful in the air.

We straightened up and looked over our shoulders at him as he came toward us. He glanced up from a clipboard in his hands, nodded in our direction, and said, " 'Morning," as if he didn't want to commit to the "Good" part. Then he stopped short, looked at the clipboard again, shook his head, and walked right into the office without saying another word.

"Hey! Didn't he see us?" Garcia asked.

"Had to," said Ippolito. "Had to."

"What's with that guy, anyway?" Wu wondered out loud.

"Creepy," somebody muttered. Then the almost-late bell rang.

"Now what?" wondered Roberto Garcia.

"What do you mean, 'now what'?" said The Schneid. "We stay here till somebody notices us."

"Not me, pal," said Planet Daley. "Davis will fry my butt if I'm late again."

"Some protest!" protested Sims. "You're willing to challenge the dress code, but you're not willing to be a couple of minutes late."

"We're not challenging the late bell," Ippolito said.

"Maybe we should," said The Schneid.

"You protest it," said Daley, heading down the hall. "I'm out of here."

"All right," said Sims. "Regroup at lunch."

"Maybe by then we can talk Wrist into going along," I pointed out.

"Be there or be square," said Ippolito.

Then we all ran for it. It was a tough call. Hall monitors considered running a capital crime. Homeroom teachers felt the same way about lateness. You were damned if you did and damned if you didn't.

"No running!" a hall monitor called out. I kept going and made a fast turn into my homeroom about four seconds after The Schneid and two seconds before the late bell.

Mrs. Corrigan, my homeroom teacher, gave me one of her dumb smiles and shook her head at The Schneid and me. "I was hoping I could start my day off with a couple of detention slips. Too bad."

I sat down just as the P.A. system started blaring the morning announcements. That exalted Lord, George Alton, tapped me on the shoulder. I turned around. "Is that zero on your shirt supposed to signify something?" he whispered.

"Yeah," I whispered back. "The total I.Q. of the Lords."

Alton flipped me the finger. I just grinned and pretended not to notice.

6

"Who asked you about yours?" Ippolito greeted me when I ran into him in the hall on the way to the cafeteria.

"A couple of teachers," I said. "A couple of kids."

"What did you tell them?"

"I tried to make up stories. Some brain-dead girl came up to me and actually said this kind of shirt went out of style last year."

"Right," said Ippolito. "Like it was the height of fall fashion two summers ago or something."

"I told her she should check out the next issue of *Seventeen*. She actually believed me. Oh, yeah, Marek said he guessed it represented the grade he was going to give me."

"Cute. A real math-teacher joke. Not bad, when all you've got on your shirt is an O. This NJ on mine means people keep making New Jersey jokes."

"I actually lived in New Jersey for a while," I pointed out.

"Was it a joke?"

"I thought it was okay. But I was about six years old. What did I know?"

We went through the line and got a couple of barfburgers and milks. Then we headed for the Official Table of the Obnoxious Jerks, which was whatever table the person who got through the line first could find. The only one there so far was Demetrios. The surprise was that he was wearing his shirt after all.

"What changed your mind?" Ippolito said.

Demetrios shrugged. "It only half changed."

He turned his back toward us. All that showed of the letters was the stitching. He was wearing the shirt inside out.

"What's the story?" I asked.

"I figured this was a gesture of solidarity. But that's as far as I go. The Schneid said nothing happened anyway."

"Well, without you it didn't exactly spell out what it was supposed to," Ippolito pointed out.

"Probably wouldn't've mattered anyway," I said, inspecting my burger for roaches. "Old Creepy definitely looks brain-dead today."

"So what now?" Demetrios asked.

"Just walk around, I guess," Ippolito said. "Or maybe try lining up here."

"Just let me know so I can get out of the way when they come get you," Demetrios said.

"And they call this food!" The Schneid said disgustedly, shaking his head and slamming his tray on the table.

"That's not what I call it," said Ippolito through a mouthful of gray meat.

"There's more plastic in the burgers than the plates," said Sims.

"Health food," said Demetrios. "So bad it puts you on a diet."

"We're definitely going to have to do something about it," said Ippolito. "There's a jerk-out in this somewhere."

"One jerk-out at a time, guys," said The Schneid. "I seem to remember something about one today. Hey, Wrist, you're with us!"

"Sort of," said Demetrios, turning his back to the newcomers.

Big groans. The Schneid tried to convince him to turn the shirt rightside out, but Wrist wouldn't go for it.

"What's the plan, fans?" Schwarzkopf asked as he sat down.

"What do you think, guys?" said Sims. "Get up on the table in the right order and make noise till somebody notices?"

"Unwise," counseled The Schneid. "Then we get tossed out for the wrong reason instead of the right one."

"Huh?" I said.

The Schneid made a face. "You're not supposed to stand on the tables. This thing would probably fall apart if we did, anyhow."

"How about the chairs?" Ippolito wondered.

Garcia and Wu arrived. "What about the chairs?" Wu asked.

"Stand up on them?" Ippolito said. "You know, to show off the shirts. Display the colors. Sooner or later somebody ought to notice."

"Anybody got the student handbook?" The Schneid asked.

"Oh, yeah," Garcia said sarcastically. "I carry that around everywhere I go."

"I just want to check and see if there's a rule about standing on the chairs," said The Schneid.

"I'm for it," said Sims.

"We're all here," Planet Daley said. "Do we go for it or not?"

"Vote?"

"All in favor, mumble 'Affirmative, Captain,'" said Sims.

Everybody did but Demetrios and Schwarzkopf. "What about you, Wrist?" Sims asked.

"Lay off, okay?" said Demetrios.

"Fine," said Sims. "What about you, Schwarzkopf?"

"I'm in."

"You didn't mumble 'Affirmative, Captain.'"

"I don't talk with my mouth full like some cretins."

"That's never stopped you before," Ippolito remarked.

Schwarzkopf stuck a tongueload of food out at him.

"Well, gentlemen," Sims said, "everybody ready?"

"Give us a break," said Wu. "We just got here."

"Yeah," Garcia agreed. "At least let us eat this trash before it gets cold and congeals into a hockey puck."

"Three minutes?" said Sims.

"Fine," Garcia and Wu agreed.

And right then Coach Arborio came up behind Harry Schwarzkopf, grabbed him by the collar, and basically whirled him around on his stool. "Very cute," Arborio said snidely.

Schwarzkopf was indignant. "Let go of me!" he demanded.

"See you, guys," said Demetrios. "Like I said, I've got to get down to the library."

"You stay put," Arborio told him, and let go of Schwarzkopf. "The rest of you, turn around."

We all improvised. Some of us twirled on our stools; others stood up and did ballet pirouettes.

"Very funny, gents," Arborio said. "We are now going to take a little trip to the principal's office."

"Why's that?" The Schneid asked.

"Oh, come on," Arborio snorted. "Let's not play innocent, gents. You know the rules."

"Are we supposed to be breaking one?" asked Wilver Sims.

"You guys." Arborio sighed. "Sometimes I just don't know."

"We'll agree with that," said Schwarzkopf, smirking.

"All right: Up, all of you. We're going down to the office."

"Why?" asked Planet Daley in mock amazement.

"I thought you were supposed to be the smart guys," Arborio sneered.

Daley laughed. "You got that right."

"Too smart for your own good," said Arborio.

"We can't imagine what you're talking about," said Ippolito.

"You know the dress code as well as anybody else," Arborio replied impatiently. "No club insignias. No uniforms."

"So what does that mean to us?"

Arborio was getting more exasperated by the minute. "You know what you're wearing."

"No, we don't," said The Schneid.

"Please tell us," said Sims.

"Gents, despite what you think about gym coaches, I do have a brain. I have a college degree. I can work out crossword puzzles. So, believe it or not, I figured out these shirts of yours. Too cute, gents, too cute. March."

We looked around the table at each other. Nobody moved. "Come on. Move it."

Sims shrugged. "Okay, men. Assume positions."

We all lined up in OBNOIOUS JEKS order. Demetrios stayed put. "You too, Demetrios. Inside-out is no excuse."

"Give me a break," Demetrios said with damp eyes that looked as though they might start weeping.

"Give *me* one," said Arborio. "And yourself. Come on."

Demetrios muttered a swear word just loud enough so you could sort of not hear it. Then he stood up, stripped off his shirt, and put it on again rightside out. "If I'm going to take gas for this, I might as well deserve it."

The rest of us cheered and hollered "Way to go, Wrist!" and a bunch of other things. Every eye in the lunchroom was suddenly focused on us. Then we marched out with the dignity that befit true OBNOXIOUS JERKS.

"Really!" said Harry Schwarzkopf sarcastically to Coach Arborio at the rear of the line. "You can actually do crossword puzzles?"

Arborio smiled and nodded tolerantly.

Harry smiled back. "You know a seven-letter word for tyrant?"

7

"We screwed up," Ippolito said glumly as we came out of detention.

"Are you kidding?" said The Schneid. "It was great! Did you see the way Old Creepy looked at us when Arborio marched us into his office?"

He was right. I laughed just thinking about it. "The best part had to be when Arborio said, 'Look,' and Crawley sort of shrugged and didn't get it, and then Arborio had to say, 'Look: See what these shirts spell out?' "

"Right," said Schwarzkopf. "And Crawley just sat there with his liverwurst sandwich on his desk and stared at us because Sims had that bright idea for everybody to scramble up the order just before we went into the office."

I grimaced, hoping nobody would remember I'd had the same problem myself when we first handed out the shirts.

"Brain-dead," said Daley, not meaning me. "Crawley

was too stupid to figure out what it spelled until Arborio rearranged us. And then he still didn't get it, because Harry kept moving out of line."

"You can bet Crawley doesn't do crossword puzzles," said The Schneid.

"It was funny, all right," Ippolito admitted. "But not the point."

"The point is, I'm only going to get killed when I get home," Demetrios said ruefully.

"The point is you know where," The Schneid told him, then turned to Ippolito. "What's your problem, Joe? I thought we got our point across pretty damn well."

"No kidding," I agreed. "First Crawley tried the argument about the club insignia, and we showed how stupid that was, since not one of us was wearing anything that even remotely resembled a club logo. Then he insisted we were wearing uniforms, and we went through the whole thing about how there wasn't anything uniform about them—all the colors were different, and no two of the shirts were alike."

"Right," The Schneid agreed. "So what did he do? He decided to discipline us on the uniform clause anyway, because all the shirts and letters were the same general style. What a joke."

"And you have to admit it really made our point when they made us wear our gym tops the rest of the day," Daley said. "I mean, that's a uniform if ever there was one. And a stupid one to boot."

"Right," said Sims. "Even in detention everybody asked why we were all wearing the gym tops when you're not supposed to wear them outside of gym."

"That's exactly it," Ippolito said. "That's *their* uniform. That's what's not the point."

"Joe, what are you trying to say?" asked The Schneid.

Ippolito was in one of his thoughtful moods. "We did okay, I guess," he admitted. "I just think we should have planned this better. We got our point across to the administration, but we didn't get it out to enough of the kids. We just looked like we were trying to sneak an Obnoxious Jerks uniform into school."

"Well, weren't we?" The Schneid inquired.

"Come on, Dennis," said Ippolito. You could always tell Ippolito was getting serious when he called you by your real first name. "*We're* not brain-dead. I mean, is there anybody here who cares at all about wearing those shirts in the school? The point was to make a statement, and we sort of blew it because we didn't do it right."

"What do you think we should have done?" Perry Wu asked.

"I don't know," Ippolito replied. "I'm not really complaining. I just know we didn't get it focused right. It was fun. Next time we'll do it better."

We had gotten to the corner where we had to turn off toward home. "Well, it'll really be fun when we get the shirts back—when did he say?—in ten days," The Schneid said.

"Fun *outside* of school," said Demetrios. "You heard what Crawley said. If he sees those shirts again once he gives them back, it's a two-day suspension."

"Dollars to donuts we'll get 'em all back but one, anyway," Sims said. "I can just see Arborio thinking it'd be a neat nasty trick."

"Yeah, right," Ippolito said. "If there's one person who would have been Lords material through and through, it's Coach Arborio."

"See you guys tomorrow," I said as Ippolito and I walked away.

"Not if we see you first!" the rest of the guys hollered. It was an Official Obnoxious Jerks Snappy Rejoinder.

"Now you want to learn the real reason we voted you into the Obnoxious Jerks?" Ippolito asked.

"What are you talking about?" I said.

39

"The real reason you got in is that if we hadn't had nine members, the shirts wouldn't have been able to spell out OBNOXIOUS."

I knew he was only kidding, but I gave him a dirty look anyway.

"All right. Lousy joke," he admitted.

"You said it," I said. "Any more cracks like that, and I may just switch over to the Lords."

"Oh, yeah, right," Ippolito said sarcastically.

Just then, George Alton breezed by on his bike, shouted a couple of obscenities, and flashed a finger at us.

"On second thought, maybe not," I said.

8

As I mentioned before, the shirts probably helped plant that brilliant skirt idea in my head, but it also had a lot to do with a girl. The girl was named Leslie Freeze. She was this tiny, skinny, fragile thing, and she always had this kind of frightened look, as though any instant something awful might happen. You can startle most people by coming up behind them and saying "Boo!" Leslie was the kind of person you could startle by walking up and saying "Hi."

Leslie was in a bunch of my classes, but the first time I actually got to know her was during the French Club's International Festival. The festival was one of the brilliant schemes of the French teacher, Mademoiselle Feldstein. It was sponsored mainly by the French Club, and if you took French, you were a member whether you wanted to be or not. If you didn't want to go to meetings after school once a week, that was okay with Mademoiselle Feldstein, but she kind of hinted that you'd get pretty lousy grades unless you did. So if you took French and you cared about your grades—and at UGH if you were taking French after your freshman year you probably did care about your grades, or at least your parents did, since the language requirement was only one year—you were probably the kind of French Club member who went to the meetings.

Sims and Garcia were in first-period French, too, but it was not one of those classes where you get to socialize much or doze off in the back. Mlle. Feldstein had a policy of calling on you when she felt like it, not when you raised your hand, and that meant you had to keep up with what was going on. If not, she'd give you this terrible harangue in French and work you over until you felt like two *centimes*.

Right around the first of the year she announced the annual International Festival. The other language clubs were participating too. The cafeteria would be decorated with international decorations. There would be international entertainment and international food. Everybody had to bring his or her parent or parents, since it was well-known that Mlle. Feldstein kept a record of who came in her infamous *petit livre noir*— that's "little black book" in French.

When Mlle. Feldstein announced she was setting up committees, the other two Obnoxious Jerks and I decided to make sure we stayed together on one. There was a finance committee, which sounded boring. There was an entertainment committee, which sounded stupid. There was a decoration committee, which sounded like a lot of work. There was a cleanup committee, which sounded puky. And there was a food committee, which sounded right up our alley. Sims, Garcia, and I put in for it and agreed to bring French dishes for the fair. We figured we'd be good at it, since by then our Connoithursdays had become so famous even La Feldstein had heard of them.

On Connoithursdays we Obnoxious Jerks basically had a picnic in the cafeteria. When Ippolito proposed it—he had to be the one who proposed it, because his parents are both amazing cooks—everybody groaned. But somehow he managed to convince us to try it, and it turned out to be our greatest running jerk-out.

Every Thursday we'd turn up with a huge table-cloth and wine glasses and something wonderful to eat. We'd show up in jackets and ties we kept in our lockers just for these special occasions. The first time we tried it, Coach Arborio was cafeteria monitor. When we un-furled the tablecloth and spread it out on the table, he looked at us as if we were going to bomb the place or something. And then the wine glasses and wine bottles totally freaked him out. "You know the rules about alcohol and drugs," he barked.

We ignored him, uncorked the bottles, and poured away. "Red or white?" Planet Daley inquired of each of us in turn.

Arborio went nuts. "That wine goes right now," he insisted as we passed it around the table. "If anybody even tastes it, it's a week's detention." Naturally, we all ignored him, raised our glasses, and clinked them to-gether in a toast to the Obnoxious Jerks. Then Planet Daley poured a glass of red and handed it with a flour-ish to our favorite coach.

"I don't want this," Arborio spluttered. "Remember, I warned you. One sip and you're out of here."

"Taste it," Schwarzkopf said. "I'm sure you'll find it amusing."

Arborio stared at him. He stared at the wine. He stared at the rest of us. We stared back.

Arborio took a deep breath. Then he tilted the glass

and took the tiniest little sip. Suddenly all the tense muscles in his face relaxed. "You guys," he said, shaking his head. "Grape juice."

"Fine year," said The Schneid. And then we set into the pasta salad Ippolito's mom and dad had made to kick off Connoithursdays. It was great.

"Everybody know what this stuff is?" Ippolito asked.

"There's some kind of weird green thing in mine," said Roberto Garcia.

"Yeah, boogers. There are boogers in mine too," said The Schneid.

"Repeat after me." Ippolito raised a forkful of food and enunciated clearly. "Ar-ti-choke heart."

"Artichoke heart," said most of the rest of us.

"Eye of newt," said Planet Daley.

"That's not the booger I meant," said The Schneid, picking at his salad. He speared a little round green thing with his fork and held it up. "This is the booger I meant."

"Repeat after me," said Harry Schwarzkopf. "Boog-er."

Ippolito made a face. "That, ignorant lads, is a caper. Repeat after me: ca-per."

"That's Italian for booger, right?" said Schwarzkopf.

Ippolito shook his head. "Ignogrunt, it comes from a bush."

"Whose?" said about half of us at once.

Ippolito sighed. "It's kind of like a pinecone or something. It's the seed of this particular plant. No big deal."

Schwarzkopf put one in his mouth and chewed it. "If it looks like a booger, it smells like a booger, and it tastes like a booger—it's a caper. Sure it is."

"Hey, lay off, guys," I said, chowing down. "This stuff is really good. You could be eating cafeteria food."

"That's an oxymoron," said Planet Daley. "A contradiction in terms."

"What is?" I asked.

"Cafeteria food."

"Right," Ippolito said. "So who's going to be responsible for next week?"

I forget who volunteered, but somehow we managed to keep it going. And then it just kind of blossomed. We had Chinese food, soul food, Irish food, Vietnamese food, Thai food, Indian food, Jewish food, you name it. Connoithursday got to be one of the high points of our week. It kind of got us over the Thursday hump. We took pride in it. Besides, it meant we didn't have to eat cafeteria food for one entire day. And it made a point about how rotten the cafeteria food really was, not that anybody did anything to make it better.

So by the time the International Festival came around and Sims, Garcia, and I took over the French food booth, we were experienced gourmets. This is where Leslie Freeze came in. She ended up joining us because there wasn't enough room on the entertainment committee. Which was a laugh, because Leslie was the last person you could imagine doing any entertaining.

We held our first committee meeting after school at French Club. "What should we have on the menu?" I asked.

"Croissants," Garcia said.

"That's not French," Sims said. "That's Burger King."

"It is so French," Garcia protested.

"Yeah, like fries," said Sims. "We need something a little more unusual. Something that'll shake people up."

"Like what?" Garcia challenged.

"Jumpin' Bean dip," I said.

Sims made a face and shook his head. "Organ meats," he stated grandly.

Leslie opened her mouth for the first time. "Organ meats?" she squeaked.

"Yeah. You know. *Foie de veau. Rognons. Ris de veau. Cervelles.* Oh, yeah. And *tête de veau.*"

"All right, show-off," said Garcia. "What is all that stuff?"

"I got one," I said. "*Tête* is head. *Veau* is veal. Calf's head, right?"

"Right," said Sims.

"Gross," said Leslie.

"Not strictly an organ," Sims admitted. "But a beautiful dish. It should, pun intended, turn some heads."

"And stomachs," I noted.

"Exactly," Sims agreed. "Let's see now. *Foie de veau:* calves' liver. *Rognons:* kidneys. *Ris de veau:* sweetbreads, which is actually the pancreas."

Leslie grabbed her stomach and made a face.

"I think I am going to throw up," said Garcia.

"They're delicious, honest," Sims claimed. "You ever have chitlins?"

Garcia made a face. "What is that?"

"Pig intestines."

"Oh, make me barf," I said.

"Come on," said Garcia. "Human beings don't eat that."

Sims brightened. "Soul food."

Leslie piped up. "Yeah. It tastes like the sole of your shoe."

I smiled at her in amazement. The thought of Leslie Freeze actually cracking a joke was a real surprise. But she didn't smile back. She just sort of shrugged.

"Kind of rubbery," Sims admitted. "And a weird tang like you wouldn't believe."

"I'd believe it," I said.

"I'm not a big fan of them myself," Sims confessed.

"And they're not all that big in France. So we'll stick to the easier stuff."

"Liver, kidney, and pancreas," I said. "And head."

"Oh, yeah, and *cervelles:* brains."

"Did you see one too many horror movies, or what?" Garcia asked.

"Brains are my personal favorite," Sims said. "Real light and airy."

"Kind of like yours," I remarked.

"Oh, yeah. I forgot one: *tripe.* In French it's pronounced 'treep.' "

Garcia nodded. "*Menudo.* I had that. Once."

"You know what it is?"

"I don't think I want to know," Garcia replied.

"It's this honeycomblike thing that's actually a cow's second stomach."

"And you want to put it in yours?" I gasped.

"It's great. Real tasty," said Sims.

"Not when I tried it," said Garcia.

"See? See how you all reacted? Think how people will go nuts when they see this stuff and we tell 'em what it is!"

"You think Mlle. Feldstein will approve this?" Leslie asked.

"Hey, she's got to," Sims said. "This is real authentic French food. French people eat this stuff. Honest."

And La Feldstein did approve it. In fact, she told us our menu was the most creative one she'd ever seen. Sims insisted it would be a masterpiece—and he was determined to make it what he called a twitch-out—kind of a mini-jerk-out, since it didn't involve our entire organization.

The afternoon of the festival, Leslie and Garcia and I were over at Wilver's house helping out. Wilver's mom was the only one who was willing to trust us with her kitchen, but he probably knew that even before he suggested the idea. He went shopping with her the night before to bring home everything we needed. Except for the calf's head. The butcher shop was out of calves' heads. Sims was really upset, because he saw that as kind of the centerpiece of our booth, but sometimes you just have to make the best of a bad situation.

A couple of things surprised me at Wilver's place. The first one was what the organ meats looked like. Seeing all that stuff in the raw was kind of like going to a horror movie where you could actually touch all the blood and guts, and I was no fan of horror movies to begin with.

The second thing, which probably shouldn't have surprised me, was what a good cook Sims was. He used the cookbook a lot, but he obviously knew what he was doing, which was more than the rest of us could say. Mostly Garcia and Leslie and I stood around and handed him things or stirred a pot when he asked us to. I was particularly impressed with the way he handled this big kitchen knife. He could chop a stalk of celery into tiny pieces in nothing flat.

"Where'd you learn all this stuff?" I asked.

"Hey, if you don't want to starve, you learn to cook. Especially when your parents aren't around all the time."

"If this is what you eat, maybe it'd be better to learn how to warm up frozen dinners," Leslie said. Actually, there was a third thing that surprised me at Wilver's place: Leslie could actually be funny. I mean, she'd made a few sharp remarks when we were planning things in French Club, but now for once in her life she didn't have her usual nervous look, and she kept coming up with these offbeat comments that were real nasty and cynical and sardonic.

"Something smells awfully good," my mom declared when she came by to take us and the food up to school.

"Your mother must be wearing really cheap perfume," Leslie remarked.

But my mom was right. Everything smelled great. As long as you didn't know what it was. Actually, it tasted pretty good too, at least the three or four samples I forced myself to try—as long as you didn't think much about what it really was. But there was just no way I was going to test out the brains.

When we got to the cafeteria, it was already decorated with lots of foreign flags and posters and stuff, but there were still people up on ladders fastening things to the ceiling. Since Mlle. Feldstein was the heavy-duty organizer of this event, the French flags and booths were near the front. Ours was right by the door—a perfect place to gross people out as they walked in. In front of our pans of food we put folded index cards. The front of each card had the French name of the food in big capital letters. The back had the English name in tiny little handwriting.

Of course, all the other Obnoxious Jerks were at the festival, too, working for the Russian Club or Spanish Club or German Club booths or one of the committees, and they dropped by our booth now and then. However, they did not agree to eat any of the food.

"What is this stuff?" The Schneid asked with a kind of screwed-up expression.

"*Délicieux*—or is it *délicieuse*?" said Sims. "Mlle. Feldstein will know. Anyhow, we have here the finest *rognons, ris de veau, foie de veau, cervelles, et tripe*"— he pronounced it "treep," of course.

"Yeah, but what *is* it?" Schwarzkopf demanded.

Garcia told him. The non–French-Club Obnoxious Jerks all made faces. The rest of us had been through it all before.

"I don't know about you guys," said Perry Wu, "but I'm going over to the German booth and check out those frankfurters."

"Me too," said Planet Daley.

"Just check back here once in a while," said Garcia, "or you'll miss the fun."

"What's the fun?" Leslie wondered.

"You'll see soon enough," said Schwarzkopf.

"Do I want to be around?" Leslie asked.

"You definitely want to be around," said Wilver Sims.

Mlle. Feldstein came over, took a look at our table, and made a kind of Crawley-like face. "Very inventive. But I wonder if this was the wisest move in economic terms."

"You just wait," said Sims. "I'll bet we have one of the most popular booths here."

"I hope you're right," she said. "It'd be a shame to let any of this go to waste."

"Want some?" Garcia asked her in French.

Mlle. Feldstein took a closer look and turned up her nose. "I'm afraid I can't. I don't eat red meat."

"Are you a vegetarian too?" Leslie asked hopefully.

"Not exactly," said La Feldstein. "I just don't eat red meat. *Bonne chance*." And she walked away.

"You're a vegetarian?" I asked Leslie.

"Pretty much. No meat or chicken. Fish and seafood once in a while."

"You don't believe in killing animals?" I asked.

Leslie shrugged. "Well, I have a leather jacket and leather shoes, so I'm not exactly dogmatic about it."

It was the first time any girl ever used a word like "dogmatic" in a conversation with me. It was really kind of neat.

"I just eat mostly vegetable and dairy products," Leslie went on. "It's supposed to be good for you."

"So you're not going to eat any of the brains either, huh?" Sims inquired.

Leslie shook her head. "The brains I was born with are fine, thanks."

"That's more than a lot of people around here can say," Schwarzkopf pointed out, gesturing toward a couple of kids coming toward our booth. One was a Lord from the junior class—a guy whose haircut was so short his ears stuck straight out from the side of his head like shriveled wings. The other was George Alton.

"Hey! Let's go! Right here!" Sims shouted at them like a carnival barker. "Most creative food on the floor! You want it, we got it."

"What is that stuff?" Bad Haircut wanted to know.

Sims gave them a grand tour of the table. "You got your *cervelles*. You got your *rognons*. You got your *foie de veau* and your *ris de veau*. You got your *tripe*. What'll it be?"

"Hey, don't give us that French crap," Alton said. "We don't take French."

"And we know why," Garcia muttered to me.

"You say you're not sure about this food? Well, hey, I'm going to give you a free sample. Now, what could be fairer than that?" Sims stuck long-handled spoons into the metal pans and dredged up some goodies. "Here you go, Alton. Here's a shot of *cervelles*. And for you, my man, we've got the *tripe*. There you go."

The two Lords looked at their plates as though there had to be a catch. "Why are you giving this stuff away?" Bad Haircut asked.

"We've got the best food at the fair," Sims said. "We just want the chance to prove it. Besides, you're our very first customers."

Alton made a face. "We hear you eat all kinds of weird stuff at that table of yours on Thursdays."

51

"Oh, we wouldn't make you eat that kind of thing," Garcia said. "Hey, eel isn't for everybody."

Bad Haircut winced. "This isn't eel, is it?"

"Nope," I said, as Leslie began to giggle behind me. "Eel it definitely is not. We personally guarantee it."

"What do you think?" Bad Haircut asked Lord Alton.

"Hey, how bad can it be?" George replied cockily.

Bad Haircut and Alton looked at each other suspiciously. Then they looked at us suspiciously. They looked at the food suspiciously. Finally they both took bites.

Sims turned our "CERVELLES" and "TRIPE" cards around to reveal the English equivalents—"calves' brains" and "tripe—a cow's second stomach."

"So tell us," he inquired, "how do you like those brains and that stomach stuff? Great, aren't they?"

Alton and Haircut had very weird expressions on their faces. They were trying to decide all at once whether the food they were eating tasted okay, whether we were telling the truth about it, and whether they should swallow it or spit it out.

It was almost too much for their mental powers, but they both went for the spit-it-out option. Haircut actually ran his index finger around his mouth to catch any stray particles he might have missed. That was even grosser than the food.

"Hey, what's the matter, guys?" Sims demanded. "We thought you Lords were tough. Hey, French women and even little kids eat brains and tripe."

"You're kidding," said Haircut. "That's not what that stuff really is."

"Look it up in any French dictionary," said Roberto Garcia. "Look it up in any butcher shop. That's what it is, all right."

"Brains?" Alton groaned.

"Some weird cow's stomach?" Haircut grunted.

"Maybe you'd like some more. Just to satisfy your-selves we're telling the truth," said Sims, handing their plates back.

"That's okay," said Haircut, pushing the food away.

"Yeah. I had plenty," said Alton.

"Always said brains and the Lords didn't agree," Sims said with a smile.

Alton got a little testy. "Wait a minute, Jerk Boy. We didn't see *you* eat that stuff."

"Anytime, sons. Anytime." Sims stuck a plastic fork in the pan, lifted a whole big hunk of brain into his mouth, chewed with great delight, and swallowed with tremendous satisfaction. "Maybe you'd rather go over there and get something more appropriate to your per-sonality," he said. "I hear the Swedish booth has meatballs."

The rest of us cracked up as Alton and Haircut slinked away. "Way to go," Garcia told Sims. The rest of us congratulated him too.

"When it comes to food, I don't fool around," Sims said. That was for sure. But it must be nice to be big enough not to have to take crap from anybody.

We managed to pull the same trick on a bunch of other kids, including a few Lords, a couple of Viscounts, and the vice president of the Student Council. It got better every time. Then people who'd been fooled started sending their friends over to our booth just to see their reactions when they found out what they were eating. That got us quite a bit of extra business. But it wasn't exactly pretty. "If I see another person spit food out into his plate, I'm going to throw up," Leslie said.

A few of the parents were the only people adventur-ous enough to eat our food once they knew what it really was. They all were pretty impressed. Ippolito's folks traded sweetbread recipes with Sims. My dad thought the kidneys were pretty good. The rest of us took his word for it.

It surprised everybody, but all in all, it turned out to be a pretty good evening. It was, that is, until everybody but the committee members had gone home and we were cleaning up our booths. For a minute Leslie and I were off to one side putting aluminum foil over the pots and pans so Sims could take them home and have leftovers. That's when Leslie hit me with the bombshell that changed my life.

"I want to join the Obnoxious Jerks," she said.

9

I didn't know what to say. I really didn't. I mean, I was the newest member of the Obnoxious Jerks. I wasn't sure what the official rules really were about new members. I suspected that when you got right down to it, there probably weren't any, since the Obnoxious Jerks weren't real fans of rules. But it didn't take even the brain of a Lord to notice that there weren't too many girls in the group. Or any.

I looked around for Garcia and Sims, but they were way over at the other end of the room, hanging out with Schwarzkopf and Demetrios at the Russian Club booth.

"Did you hear me?" Leslie asked.

"I heard you," I said. "Why do you want to join?"

Leslie smiled. "I like you guys."

"Yeah?" I said, kind of vamping for time. I still had no idea how to handle the situation.

"I had fun tonight. You guys are really smart. You're funny. You do things to upset the status quo around here, and God knows, it sure can use a lot of upsetting."

I shrugged. "Glad somebody noticed."

"So I'd like to join," she said eagerly. "I'd like to be a part of that."

"Great. I'm flattered. But why are you asking me?"

"Who should I ask?"

"I'm not even sure. But I'm the last one who'd be able to tell you that kind of thing. I don't even know what our rules are about that. I'm new around here, remember?"

"Maybe that's kind of why I asked you," Leslie mumbled, looking away.

Then I said something I probably shouldn't have. "Look, I'll find out for you. I'll see what we do about new members."

"Honest?" She gave me this look that was kind of skeptical but at the same time so intense and eager I couldn't resist it.

"Honest. I promise. Scout's honor. Obnoxious Jerk's honor." I raised my hand to make the scout's honor sign and wiggled my fingers around in a slightly goofy way.

She sort of half-giggled. Some of her nervousness had come back. "Okay," she said. We finished putting the foil on the pans, and her mother came through the door. A second later Leslie disappeared.

Of course, I could have asked somebody about the rules right there and then. Most of the Obnoxious Jerks were still in the cafeteria. It wouldn't have been a big deal to say something like "Guess who just said she wanted to join the Obnoxious Jerks!" and find out how everybody reacted.

Or at least it shouldn't have been a big deal. But somehow I couldn't bring myself to do it. I didn't know exactly why. I think it was because I was afraid I'd bring up the subject and about ten seconds later hear uproarious laughter at poor Leslie's expense.

So I waited until Ippolito and I were walking to

school next day and told him what Leslie had asked. "That's a new one!" he snorted. "She really said that? Leslie 'Iceberg' Freeze?"

"Did you make that nickname up just now?" I asked.

"Are you kidding?"

"Well, how come I never heard it before?"

"Because she isn't exactly a major topic of conversation. And the last time anybody used it in front of her, she burst out in tears. Not quite the same as with you, Back. Or Planet, or The Schneid."

"Interesting," I admitted. "But what about my question?"

"I didn't think you asked a question. I thought you just told me Leslie Freeze wanted to join the Obnoxious Jerks."

"Okay. The question is what you think about that idea."

Ippolito looked thoughtful. "Not much. What do you think about it?"

"I can't make up my mind what I think about it. I mean, I don't know her all that well. Or the group."

"Well, for one thing, you don't ask to get into the Obnoxious Jerks. We ask you."

"It's not as though she made a formal request or anything," I said. "She just said she'd like to be a member."

"Lots of people would like to be members who aren't."

"Yeah? Like who?"

"Omar Gormley."

"Omar Gormley? The school's worst nerd? You're kidding!"

"Ask him if I'm kidding. On second thought, don't. It would reopen some painful wounds."

"How do you know Omar Gormley wants to join the Obnoxious Jerks?"

"Same way you know Leslie Freeze wants to."

"He told you?"

"Not me. He told Wu. Wu was his lab partner in biology last year."

"So what happened?"

"Perry proposed him for membership. It was pretty awful. We ended up spending a whole meeting trying to decide what we should do."

"Why so long?"

"It was a question of philosophy. These things get complicated."

"What kind of philosophy?" I asked.

"Look, we're the Obnoxious Jerks. We don't stand for what other people stand for, right?"

"Obviously."

"I mean, the whole point is that we're too smart to stand for stupidity. Not silly stupidity—you know, the kind of thing we do in the jerk-outs to make a point—but real absolute unintentional stupidity, which is most of what happens around this school. People call us antiauthority, but that's not totally true. We're not the heavy-metal crowd or the drug crowd or the get-drunk-and-puke-on-beer crowd, and in a way you could call all of them antiauthority. But they're all stupid. What we're against is *stupid* authority. Right?"

I nodded. "Gotcha. But what does all that have to do with Omar Gormley?"

"Well, we try to practice what we preach—excuse the giant cliché. We try not to act like stupid authority ourselves. That's why we don't have an official president or a chairman or any of that stuff. We try to do everything by—what's the word?—consensus."

"I still don't get it."

"You know how the Lords and Viscounts act all high-and-mighty? Like they'd be doing you a tremendous favor to let you join their ultraselective club, and implying that you're something incredibly special just for being allowed the exalted privilege of getting in? We don't go in for all that garbage."

"I know. That's one of the reasons I joined."

"The problem is there's another side. Do you let everybody in, or do you make choices? Do you turn it into just another group, with rules and regulations and elections and all that crap, or do you leave it as a bunch of friends who think pretty much the same way about things? Do you bring in every nerd who thinks he's like you? It's a tough call."

I could see what he was talking about. "Man! I never thought about any of that stuff. It's not easy, is it?"

"It sure isn't. Hey, nobody wants to be mean to Omar. He's okay. He's just terminally boring. And the other whole point of the Obnoxious Jerks is to hang out with interesting people, people you feel comfortable with. Tell me anybody feels comfortable with Omar Gormley. Except maybe one of his nerdy friends."

I couldn't come up with even one name.

"When we had this meeting about Gormley, some-body—I think it was Sims, oddly enough—made the argument that if we have to let everybody in, what are we going to do when some Lord wants to join, just to be a real jerk about it? It'd destroy the whole thing. So in the end most of us voted to table Omar's nomination, which meant we kept him out. I didn't exactly feel proud of it, but I voted that way myself."

I sighed. "Not much chance for Leslie, is there?"

"You want the realistic answer?"

"No," I said sarcastically. "I want science fiction."

"The realistic answer is that Leslie Freeze doesn't have a snowball's chance in hell."

"Because she's a girl?"

"Hey, we don't have anything against girls." He leered, did a Groucho Marx imitation, and said, "There are plenty of girls I'd like to have something against."

"Yeah, right. 'If I said you had a beautiful body, would you hold it against me?'" I was quoting a not-very-good country song.

"There you go." Ippolito laughed.

"Then how come we don't have any girl members?"

"It's the girls who have stuff against us. Remember the way some of them acted the day we pulled off the shirt jerk-out?"

"All right, so a couple of them called us morons and stuff. That doesn't count. They're mostly Lordettes anyway."

"But it's typical. That's how all the girls look at us. No sense of humor."

"Obviously that's not the way Leslie looks at us. She told me how much fun she had hanging around the booth."

"Sure—when we were all on our best behavior because there were teachers around. What's she going to think when we start getting really crude, slinging the swear words and dirty jokes and stuff?"

"You *are* saying it. You're saying you don't want girls in the Obnoxious Jerks. You don't want Leslie to join because she's a girl."

"No," Ippolito said firmly. "You want the real truth? The whole Chipirito?"

"No. I want all lies."

"You're getting the truth: I don't want her to join because she's Leslie Freeze."

I scowled at him.

Ippolito sighed. "Look, put the question of whether girls should join the Obnoxious Jerks aside for a minute. I don't see much of Leslie this year, since I think the only class I have with her is social studies, so maybe she has some kind of great redeeming feature I'm missing. Though it isn't her body, I can tell you that."

"I didn't think we were talking about making her

Miss America or even Miss Obnoxious Jerk. I thought we were talking about making her a member."

"Okay. Just ask yourself one question. This is all that matters: If Leslie were a guy, would you want her in the Obnoxious Jerks?"

I stalled. I thought about it. I couldn't decide. I mean, I just didn't know her that well. I remembered what Ippolito had said about Perry Wu and his shyness and how they finally figured out he was okay. Maybe it would work out the same way with Leslie. "I'm not sure," I said.

"Okay," Ippolito said. "Nomination tabled. When you're sure, you'll know it."

"Fair enough."

"And then if you want to bring her up for membership, fine. But we'll need plenty of Chipiritos, because I can tell you for sure, that is going to be one long, long meeting."

That was pretty much where we left it. Now all I had to do was break the news to Leslie. All I had to do! After Ippolito's reminder, I wasn't sure she wouldn't break into tears the instant I told her. I also wasn't sure just what the news was. So I just kind of tried to avoid thinking about it until I had a chance to sort it all out. Unfortunately she cornered me first thing Monday morning on the way into French.

"Did you find out?" she asked with this kind of breathless air of expectation, as though she expected I would tell her something absolutely terrific.

"Yeah," I said as cheerfully as I could under the circumstances.

"Yes? Does that mean I can join?"

I tried to keep up a jokey tone. "You still want to? You didn't sleep on it and reconsider?"

"Give me a break. Why?"

"Lots of people would give you lots of reasons. The Obnoxious Jerks don't exactly win popularity contests."

"Yeah. I noticed."

I tried to stall for time. "Let's talk about it after class, okay? I've got to look over my notes before La Feldstein pulls *un truc sale*."

"Is that really the idiomatic usage for 'dirty trick'?" Garcia asked as he pushed past us into the classroom.

"Idiotic is more like it," I said. "But it's just the kind of thing Feldstein has been known to pull."

"Okay," Leslie said. "After class." She may have looked breathless before, but now she looked as though somebody had knocked the wind right out of her.

I nodded. So all I had to do all through class was figure out how I was going to put it to her—and try not to daydream so much I'd bring the wrath of La Feldstein down on me. By the time class ended, I had managed to survive Feldstein's daily grilling, except for one stupid masculine-feminine mix-up. But I still didn't have any great ideas about what I was going to tell Leslie.

"So . . ." Leslie said with the look people get when they expect to hear bad news.

"It's kind of complicated," I said, still trying to think of a good way to phrase it.

"What's complicated about it? It's either yes or no."

"Hey, you know that's not true. You've got Allander for history. Nothing's either yes or no."

Leslie looked frustrated. "Great. So is it mostly yes or mostly no?"

"I told you. It's kind of complicated."

"And I told you it can't be."

If she only knew. "I asked. What they said is basically—I don't know how to put this without sounding snotty—that we invite new members. Members don't invite themselves."

"So why can't somebody invite me now that they know I'm interested?"

"I told you, it's not that easy."

Leslie's eyes kind of moistened over, and there was a sort of catch in her voice. "And why is that?"

"I don't understand all the details. But basically our philosophy is—I mean, this is what I was told anyway—that when somebody's right for the Obnoxious Jerks, we'll know it."

"What? Do you get some kind of sign from above?"

I made a face. "We just know, that's all." Leslie's damp eyes kept staring at me. "At least that's what they told me."

"Who's 'they'?" she said in an angry tone. "Joe Ippolito?"

I didn't know why she was mentioning his name, but it didn't matter much anyway. I sighed. "Look, I'm sorry."

"Okay. Okay," she said. "No problem." And she walked past me and down the hall.

"Hey, new girlfriend?" Sims asked me when I sat down beside him in Marek's class about three seconds before the bell rang.

"What?" I said.

"You know who I'm talking about. La Freeze."

"Give me a large economy-size break," I said. Girlfriend? I didn't even know if she was my friend, period. Hell, I could understand it if right at this moment she actually hated my guts.

10

For a long while Leslie and I sort of avoided talking to each other. It wasn't official or anything. I guess it was just that we both felt kind of embarrassed about what had happened.

And in a way I began to think Ippolito was right about her. The sense of humor she'd showed at the International Festival seemed to be a total fluke. She went back to being kind of distracted in class. A few times La Feldstein nailed her for talking to herself. "I don't know who your imaginary friend is back there, Freeze," she snapped in French after tossing a *crayon* in Leslie's direction, "but it had better not be somebody who only speaks English."

So Leslie didn't get invited to join the Obnoxious Jerks, and I couldn't honestly say that was wrong. Things were going okay for our band of brains. Why rock the boat?

Then came the infamous UGH Talent Show. We

had a great jerk-out planned for this one. The only problem was that we had to get by an audition committee to get into the show, and the audition committee was just loaded with Lords and Viscounts. We held our rehearsal at my place.

"No problem," said Schwarzkopf as he opened up his violin case. "We've got it made in the shade."

"I don't know," I said, plunking my banjo. "Maybe we're not that good."

"This man," said Ippolito, pointing to me as he tuned his mandolin, "has never sat through one of the patented UGH talent shows. He does not understand the meaning of the term 'bad.' "

" 'Putrid' is more like it," said Wilver Sims, balancing the bow of his bass on the tip of his finger.

"What are you guys talking about?" I asked.

"I try to block it out of the old memory," said Schwarzkopf, "but it keeps coming back. Ow, how it keeps coming back. Last year we had this senior who sang what she called opera. We called it the 'Screech Owl Aria.' "

"You had to hear it to believe it," Ippolito said. "Too bad she won't be around this year."

"Maybe she will be," said Sims. "If there's any justice, she should've flunked music."

"Remember the tap dancer who ran out of breath by the time she finished?" said Ippolito. "Up there on the stage gasping and coughing and wheezing? Not a pretty sight."

"I think she was a junior," Sims said. "You may be in luck, Back."

"Then we had the three rock bands who knew about one chord each," Schwarzkopf went on. "Oh, yeah, and our sensitive folk singer—you know Donna Kerness?"

"The one on Student Council?" I said.

Schwarzkopf nodded.

"The one who always wears all those expensive clothes and has her makeup absolutely perfect?"

"That's the one," said Sims.

I can't exactly explain it, but Donna Kerness was not the kind of person you could imagine being up there with a guitar. "She sings folk music?"

"Worse," Ippolito said. "She *writes* folk music. Quite possibly the lamest rhymes in the world. You can just bet she'll be around for more."

"Dancers who can't dance, singers who can't sing, actors who can't act, comedians who can't tell jokes. And those are the ones who got past the audition committee. Of course, some of those were friends of the committee members," Schwarzkopf pointed out, "but I'm telling you, Back, we've got nothing to worry about."

"If we can come up with an audition piece," I said.

"All we have to do is play something good enough to fool them," said Sims with a fiendish gleam in his eye. "Then we shall have our revenge!"

Ippolito and I looked at each other. "You other guys know any Bill Monroe tunes?" he asked.

Sims and Schwarzkopf gave us blank looks.

"Bill Monroe? The father of bluegrass?" I asked.

"My tastes run more to jazz. Ron Carter," Sims said.

"Did any of you cretins ever hear of a cool dude named Mozart?" Schwarzkopf asked.

"We've heard of him, all right," I said. "But last I heard, he didn't write for mandolin and banjo."

"Mandolin, maybe. Banjo, no," Schwarzkopf admitted. "Just my luck to hook up with guys who can only play low-rent instruments."

"Okay, gang," said Ippolito. "It's Bill Monroe. Sims, it'll be jazzy enough that you can keep up with us—don't give me that look, Wilver, it's true. The big question is you, Schwarzkopf. You know anything about country fiddle?"

Schwarzkopf put the violin under his chin and rattled off a pretty fair rendition of "Turkey in the Straw."

"Maybe we do have a chance, at that," I said.

We practiced Bill Monroe's "Jerusalem Ridge" for a whole afternoon, and a couple of days later we just wowed the audition committee. True, Joe and I choked up a little and didn't exactly hit every note, but Sims was rock-steady down there on the bass, and Schwarzkopf was so soulful in the high fiddle part that our screwups didn't matter a bit.

"If we wanted to, we could polish that piece a little more and win with it," Schwarzkopf said as he put his fiddle back in its case. "Particularly if you guys on the frets could manage to hit, say, fifty percent of the notes."

"That's not the plan," Sims reminded him. "This was just a preliminary so we can get on stage for our jerk-out."

"I was just saying 'if,' " Schwarzkopf replied. "Purely hypothetical. Hey, everybody else is likely to be so terrible even our jerk-out might win."

The talent show was a UGH tradition, which meant everybody in the school knew how awful it would probably be. It was also a mandatory assembly, which meant everybody had to show up.

When we arrived backstage, somebody I dimly remembered from the audition committee went around to hand out performance schedules. Our act was set for fairly late in the show. And then I noticed who was going to follow us: Leslie Freeze.

"What's she going to do?" I wondered.

"She's your pal, buddy," said Ippolito. "You're the one who should know."

I looked around. I didn't see Leslie anywhere. I figured she must be on the other side of the stage someplace.

"Hey, check this out," said Sims, pointing to the stage.

Mrs. Jackman, the guidance counselor, came out to the mike and reminded the audience that everyone on the program had worked long and hard. In the tradition of UGH respect and civility she hoped there would be no booing or hissing.

"This is an exhibition, not a competition," Schwarzkopf muttered as we watched from the wings. "Please: No wagering."

Then the UGH Cheer Team came out, with the leggy girls in their short skirts all looking adorable. And untouchable, unless you happened to be a Lord. Of course all the male cheerleaders were Lords, every last one of them. When a couple of them picked up girls and raised them high above their heads, Schwarzkopf said, "Look at that guy, he's staring right up—oh, no, stop me, I can't look anymore, I'm going to faint."

The cheerleaders were an exhibition, not part of the competition; just something to warm the audience up. Their routine featured the music of "Roll On, Griswold," the fight song so near and dear to every member of our school's brain-dead constituency. The Cheer Team was actually pretty good as cheerleaders go, but the four of us could not keep from smirking and cracking up. We had a thing about "Roll On, Griswold" that afternoon.

The opening act was a fat senior girl opera singer. I am not exactly the person to judge that stuff, but Schwarzkopf knows opera upside down, which is exactly how he thought the screechy singer should be hung before being boiled in a vat of oil. Then came a rock band called the Tall Trolls. They were so good half the audience was holding its ears by the time they finished.

Next a couple of senior girls got up there and did a ventriloquist act so bad that the way you could tell the humans from the dummies was the humans moved their mouths more. Then, as promised, or maybe "threatened" is the right word, came Donna Kerness. She accompanied herself on her guitar with some endless song she had written about how the birds were dying and the children were crying. I don't know about the birds and the children, but it was all we Obnoxious Jerks could do to keep from laughing.

I looked at my schedule. There was a long, long way to go before we got on. I was feeling kind of nervous and fidgety, so I decided to stroll around backstage.

I spotted Leslie standing near the back wall. She was talking to herself again, mouthing words and making gestures. She was so into whatever it was she was doing that when I came over, she jumped back, startled. Or maybe that was just her usual nervous reaction.

"Hey, it's just me," I reminded her.

Leslie gave me an exasperated look. "Thanks," she said sarcastically. "You just broke into my rehearsal."

"Sorry," I said, drawing back. "See you later."

She sighed. "Oh, stick around. I've only rehearsed this thing about eighty-nine times. If I don't know it now, I never will."

"You're on right after us. Tough act to follow."

I was just making conversation, but Leslie took me seriously. "Oh, God, I hope not. What are you guys doing?"

"Top secret," I said. "How about you?"

Leslie shrugged. "Me too."

"You with anybody?" I asked.

"What do you mean?" She started biting the nail on her left index finger. I noticed there wasn't a whole lot left to bite.

"You know," I said. "With your act. Is anybody with you?"

"Me, myself, and I."

"Singing?"

Leslie shook her head.

"Dancing?"

"Come on. You'll see soon enough."

There didn't seem to be anything else to say, so I wished Leslie good luck.

She shook her head. "Don't you know anything? Break a leg."

I made a face. "What?"

"What you say in the theater is 'Break a leg.' It's bad luck to wish people good luck."

"Where'd you hear that?"

"Where'd I have to hear it?" she said irritably. "It's true. I'm not making it up."

"I believe you. I take it back. Forget the good luck." It sounded weird, but what did I know? "Break a leg."

"You too."

Schwarzkopf came over to get me. "Come on. Quick! You've got to see this."

I kind of waved good-bye to Leslie and followed Schwarzkopf to the wings, where the rest of our crew was waiting. He pointed to the stage. There was a group lip-synching to the latest rap record. Except they weren't in synch and they had all the moves of a handicapped snail.

"Now that's talent!" Schwarzkopf said, half-shouting to make himself heard over the music.

"Hey, it's better than most of the acts," Ippolito pointed out. "At least the music is halfway in tune."

"If you call that music," said Sims.

"How much more of this do we have to endure?" I wondered.

"Hey, you missed the ballet," Schwarzkopf said. "A couple of senior girls hopping around in their tutus. Tutu much."

"What next?" I wondered.

"More agony and pain, no doubt," said Schwarzkopf.

"What's old Leslie up to back there?" Sims wanted to know.

"She's on after us," I said.

"What's she doing?" Schwarzkopf asked.

"Won't tell me. All I know is she's going it alone."

"Leslie? High-strung Leslie up there all by her lonesome? You've got to be kidding?"

I shrugged. "I only know what she told me."

"Maybe it's some kind of marionette act or something," Ippolito said. "You know, something where she can kind of hide behind the backdrop."

"I don't think so," I said. "I didn't see any props back there."

"Well, you can bet one thing. She's really going to have a tough time following our little extravaganza," Ippolito said.

"Yeah," Sims agreed. "I just hope those guys haven't dozed off out there in the audience."

"Dozed off?" Schwarzkopf said. "We'll be lucky if they haven't walked out."

"How many more acts till we're on?"

Ippolito consulted the list. "Five, I think. No, make that four."

So we watched a junior girl who thought she was Barbra Streisand. Nobody else did. We heard a classical pianist who Schwarzkopf said had a lot less talent than the guys who wheeled the piano on stage. We put our hands over our ears for another rock band that confused loud with good. Then a group of kids who did something from Shakespeare did a nice job of starting snide conversations among the half of the audience that was still awake.

When I heard Mrs. Jackman say "Let's have a nice hand for the Renaissance Players" and saw the stagehands rearranging the mikes, I got that strange feeling you get in your throat when you're about to go on stage.

I gulped a couple of times and took a couple of deep breaths, but the feeling wouldn't go away.

Then Mrs. Jackman said, "And now you're in for a real treat," which she had said about every act that went up on stage, except Donna Kerness, who she must have seen before. "Please put your hands together for the Four Country Sophomores."

We looked at each other, nodded, and strode forward. Showtime!

11

We went on stage in a dignified way. We bowed to the smattering of applause from the five Obnoxious Jerks in the audience. We adjusted our microphones. We tuned up our instruments.

Ippolito counted, "A-one, a-two, a-three." We reached into our pockets, took out kazoos, and burst into a buzzy, nasal, farty, off-key rendition of "Roll On, Griswold," the fight song so near and dear.

At first some of the brain-dead kids in the audience actually cheered us. They must have thought we were upholding the honor of the school or something. But as we bent the notes and the tune turned sourer and sourer, some hissing and hooting and outright booing broke out. A perfectly aimed rotten tomato hit Sims square in the forehead. Another one spattered all over the stage.

The booing got louder. A third tomato arced down and just missed me. Dodging a whole volley of rotten red missiles, we held our instruments behind us to protect them. But we kept the kazoos in our mouths and valiantly played on.

The tomatoes stopped. Suddenly we saw something even worse. In shock we all opened our mouths and let our kazoos fall to the floor. Ten seconds later each of us received a wet, gooey lemon meringue pie in the face. The culprits hollered "Sic semper tyrannis!" as they ran down the aisles and out the doors.

The auditorium turned to bedlam. About half the audience was laughing at the total craziness of the scene. Another sizable bunch was booing wildly. Some teachers were shouting "Get them!"—meaning the pie throwers—and some kids started hollering "Yeah! Get them!"—meaning us.

We retained our dignity. We picked up our kazoos, strode majestically to the microphones, and played the final notes of the Merrie Melodies theme. "That's all, folks," we said in unison. Exit stage left.

The crowd went wild. There was booing, hissing, hollering, and even a little applause. Mrs. Jackman took the mike and tried to calm things down. She definitely had her work cut out for her.

In the wings Leslie was waiting to go on. She was breathing deeply, shaking her head slowly back and forth, and muttering, "Damn! Damn!"

"What did you think?" I asked.

"You planned the whole thing, didn't you?" Leslie demanded. "The tomatoes, the pies, everything. Right?"

I shook my head. "Not me personally."

"You knew I was going on after you," she said angrily. "You might have told me, so I'd know what to expect."

"We couldn't give it away beforehand," I tried to explain. "That would've spoiled everything."

"Damn!" she muttered to herself, still shaking her head nervously. "Damn!"

"Hey, it's going to be okay," I said. "Break a leg."

"Go to hell," she told me.

The crowd was finally settling down. Mrs. Jackman insisted that the school would not tolerate any more outbursts like this and that the persons responsible would be disciplined severely. A couple of sarcastic hoots of "All right!" greeted that news.

Mrs. Jackman tried to ignore them. She got back into her mistress of ceremonies voice again and said, "We have another special act from the sophomore class."

"Wasn't that last one enough?" someone shouted from the audience.

Mrs. Jackman pretended not to hear. "Ladies and gentlemen," she said. "Leslie 'The Iceberg' Freeze!"

Hearing Mrs. Jackman read the nickname nobody had the guts to use to Leslie's face was a real surprise. We could tell it was a surprise to Mrs. Jackman, too, from the way she raised her eyebrows when she read it.

" 'The Iceberg'?" Schwarzkopf said loud enough for Leslie to hear. I could tell she heard, but she didn't bother to answer. She was concentrating hard.

Leslie didn't rush out the minute she heard her name. She just sort of stood there in the wings and took deep breaths and waited for Mrs. Jackman to walk off the stage. Then she waited a second or two longer—just long enough for somebody in the crowd to holler, "Let's go!"

She took one more deep breath. And she went. Schwarzkopf gave me a look and started saying something. I put my finger to my mouth to shush him. I wanted to see this.

Leslie stood at the front of the stage and calmly adjusted one of the mikes. There were a couple of hoots from the audience, but she didn't pay them the least bit of attention. She just kind of swayed back and forth until she was good and ready. Then she leaned into the mike, looked all around the audience, and made a kind of contemptuous, disgusted face. "So this is the big time!" she sort of snarled. A couple of kids laughed.

"I was going to come out here and ask if everybody was having fun," Leslie said in an arrogant tone. "But after seeing all those acts, I realize the only reason you're still in those seats is that you can chew gum there in the dark and you can't in class." There were a few more laughs from the audience.

She took a stick from her pocket and held it up. "The drug of our generation." A couple more laughs.

She unwrapped the gum, put it in her mouth, and made big cowlike motions with her jaws. "Yum," she said. "Delicious." Chewing and slurping away, she looked incredibly satisfied with herself.

I don't know how she did it, but suddenly Leslie turned herself into a teacher. "Miss Freeze, come here," she said sternly. I mean, she really looked and moved like a teacher.

And then just as suddenly she turned back into herself chewing the gum and slurping and carrying on. Only it wasn't herself. It was some mythical, typical gum-chewing student we all recognized somehow. The student pointed to herself and mouthed the word "Me?" as though she didn't understand what the teacher could possibly be talking about. The crowd started to giggle.

Leslie turned back into the teacher again. "No," she said sarcastically. "The person behind you."

With a satisfied grin she turned back into the gum-chewer and relaxed as though the teacher had really meant what she'd said. Laughs came louder and harder from the audience. Lightning-quick, the student became the teacher again.

Teacher: "Miss Freeze!"

Still chewing away, the student pointed to herself and mouthed "Me?" again.

Teacher: "Yes! You!"

The student made a frustrated face. "Huh?"

Teacher: "Take that gum out of your mouth! Now!"

Very annoyed, the student slowly stretched out a big pink wad of gum.

Teacher: "Now put it on your nose!"

The student made a face, pointed to herself and mouthed "Me?" one more time.

Teacher, sarcastically: "No, the person in front of you."

The student reached forward with the gum and started to put it on the nose of the imaginary person in front of her. The audience roared.

Teacher: "You! Put it on your own nose! Right now!"

The student took the wad of gum, slapped it right on the middle of her nose, and made a nasty face at the teacher. Then she took a chunk of the gum off her nose and stuck one hunk up one nostril so that it looked like a booger hanging down.

The audience groaned and shouted, "Gross!" Leslie gave them a big smile and stuck an even bigger hunk up her other nostril. "You said put it on my nose!" The crowd roared again.

The student pulled the gum off her nose and tossed it into the audience. Some girls in the front row shrieked and separated as if the gum were a mouse or something. "Hey, you, down there," Leslie said, turning back into herself—well, not herself, actually, but a confident version of herself I didn't really recognize. "It's only chewed-up gum. It's not something terrible—like your grade point average."

Schwarzkopf and the rest of us nearly fell on the floor over that one. And Leslie really had the crowd in the palm of her hand now.

"All right," she said, snapping the mike off its stand and prowling around the stage. "What's—wrong—around

—here?" She said it defiantly, each word separate from the other, like a sarcastic cheer. She was herself again, or at least this sneering, snotty new self nobody'd ever seen before.

"What do you really want out of life?"

She jumped to the right and turned into this brainless bimbo with a high breathy voice and big insincere smile and sort of slow, sexy moves. "I want to be popular."

Jump to the left—sneering again. "Popular? You? Give me a break!"

Right, nodding calmly: "I want to be the most popular person in the entire school."

Left, with nasty look toward the right: "From what I hear, you've been working on it."

Right, with big smile: "The whole football team thinks I'm a very generous individual."

Left: Not one word. Just a look that says, "Yeah, I'll bet."

Right, with a lazy, sexy yawn and stretch and a big nod: "And then there are those Lords . . ."

Left: "You're definitely their type."

Right, with lots of self-satisfaction: "Yes. An inte . . . uh, inter . . . intel-lectual."

Left, with a nasty nod: "Yeah, I've seen you down at Burger King. 'Ooh, this cash register is so complicated. Which button do I press for the Whopper?' "

Right, with an indignant look: "It's confusing. The Whopper and the Bacon Cheese look almost exactly the same, and they're both very, very popular."

Left: "Exactly like you, dear."

Right, with a big smug self-satisfied smile and nod.

Left, with a sneer: "Exactly like you. Your highest goal is to resemble a piece of meat."

Right, with a kind of confused look.

Left, imitating the bimbo: "Sorry. I left out the buns."

Right scowled, then preened. By now the audience was just blown away.

Suddenly Leslie was back to her good old own self—or rather that new self she was presenting on the stage. "All right, gang. Remember Simon Says?"

A couple of "Yeah"'s and "Sure"'s from the audience.

"Okay. You ready?"

A couple of "Yeah"'s and a couple of "Ready"'s.

"Simon says all the men put your hands on your head." Leslie put her hands on her head.

A few of the kids in the audience did too, but most of them didn't. "Come on, guys! What are you, chicken or something?" Leslie said. "This is high-class entertainment! You there in the front row! I said all the men put hands on their heads. Are you a man, or a boy? Hands up!"

More of the guys put their hands on their heads. "All right," Leslie said. "Good. Now, all the women pick the men's pockets." She got her biggest laugh yet.

Leslie pointed toward the audience. "You there . . . yeah, you, the cheerleader with the hands in that guy's pocket. . . . Yeah, you! Get 'em out of there! I didn't say 'Simon says.'" Another roar.

"And you there, big fellow—Simon didn't say hands down off your head, either." She roamed to the other side of the stage. "All right. *Simon says* all the women pick the men's pockets." Another big laugh.

"All right. Now it gets tough. Simon says try and get the classes you want. Simon says say something positive about the social situation in this school. Simon says try and get an education without killing yourself."

She stopped the rapid-fire attack. "You're not doing anything Simon said. Simon's getting fed up with you."

The crowd laughed. "All right. Here's the toughest one of all. You ready?"

There were some shouts from the audience.

79

"You. Did I say take those hands down from your head?" More laughs.

"Okay. Now for the tough one. Simon says eat the cafeteria food."

The audience howled. Leslie reached into her pocket and tossed a couple of sticks of gum into the audience. Then she took a bow, flipped a finger to the crowd—her index finger, I noticed—and strutted off.

The reaction was incredible. It wasn't the polite applause everybody else had gotten or the hoots we had heard. She really had won the crowd over.

"She's in," I said to Ippolito over the roar as Leslie rushed past and headed for the far corner backstage. If that performance didn't qualify her to be an Obnoxious Jerk, what would?

I started over to congratulate her, tell her how great she was. But halfway there I could hear a sort of familiar noise, and I slowed down a bit.

"We'll see," Ippolito told me. Over in the corner Leslie was throwing up.

12

It wasn't pretty. It was bad enough that Leslie was puking her guts out, but her body was shaking, too, shuddering, sobbing. I wanted to tell her how great I thought she'd been, but it was not exactly the perfect moment. In fact, she was waving one hand behind her as if she wanted people just to go away and leave her alone.

I just stood there. I figured she might want some help or something, though I didn't exactly have any great ideas about what I could possibly do. So I just stood there till she was all puked out.

She finished shaking and shuddering and took a tissue out of her pocket. Then she turned and saw me standing there and came up with this amazingly sheepish grin. "I wasn't kidding," she said. "Damn that cafeteria food."

I laughed. She wiped her mouth again and shook her head and sighed.

"Very funny," said a stern, humorless voice behind me that didn't see one bit of humor in the situation. Creepy Crawley tapped me on the shoulder. "You. Let's go."

I turned around and saw the other three members of our band behind him. "Me?" I protested. "Why me?"

"You know why," he said. "You and your friends are all going for a visit in my office. And you, young lady—we'll be discussing your performance a bit later."

"If it matters, we all thought it was pretty terrific," Schwarzkopf said.

"If she doesn't win the prize, there's no justice," I added.

"Hey! Don't forget *our* act!" Sims joked.

"She isn't going to win the prize," said Crawley, "because she's been disqualified."

"Disqualified?" a couple of us said at the same time. We noticed that Leslie was smiling and nodding and shrugging.

"Right," Crawley said. "The same reason you were. She didn't give the performance she auditioned. We do have rules, you know."

"Boy, do we ever," muttered Schwarzkopf.

"Just wanted to give folks a little surprise," Leslie said sheepishly in a tiny voice. As she ran her tongue around her mouth with distaste, we could see her slowly turning back into the Leslie we all knew before we found out this other Leslie even existed.

"That's not the way we do things here at Griswold," said Crawley.

"That's for sure," said Schwarzkopf. "It was actually funny."

"Let's go," said Crawley. "You're keeping your cohorts waiting."

"Our what?" Ippolito demanded with a very believable air of amazement.

"You know who I'm talking about," Crawley said. "And if you don't, you'll find out in my office. Now, move."

We moved. I shot Leslie a glance over my shoulder. Either she didn't see or she didn't want to respond. At the moment she was sitting on a trunk, sighing and wiping the vomit from her shoes.

When we got to Crawley's office, it was crawling with Obnoxious Jerks. It was like an unofficial meeting. The guys were sitting on the chairs and sprawled across the desk. The only one missing was Wrist Demetrios, who had been afraid of the whole deal and decided to work undercover.

Demetrios was the one who had supplied the pies. His uncle or cousin or somebody ran a diner way out on the Pike, and he was able to get the pies dirt cheap. They were great pies too. In a way, it was a shame to waste them. I still had some lemon meringue on my shirt pocket. I suspected it might come in handy. Our Chipirito-filled official meeting, scheduled for that afternoon, was likely to get started kind of late.

No doubt about it: When it came to handling us, Crawley was way out of his league. He was used to dealing with serious problems—the usual band of drug dealers, beer drinkers, cigarette smokers, punch-out artists, airheads, flunk-outs, neurotics, suicides. He didn't see smart kids much, except to give them achievement awards, and he probably liked it that way.

First he told Garcia to get off his desk and The Schneid to get out of his chair. They did. But when he sat down, he suddenly realized he was surrounded by a roomful of Obnoxious Jerks standing around, not counting Daley and Wu in the two chairs opposite the desk, so he stood up again. Apparently he didn't like being towered over when it came time to crack the whip.

"All right," he said wearily. "What are we going to do with you wise guys?"

We didn't make it easy on him by offering suggestions. "Excuse me, sir," said Roberto Garcia, raising his hand. The way Garcia said "sir" made perfectly clear that it was not intended with the least bit of respect.

"Yes?" Crawley said irritably.

"What is the accusation against us, sir? What terrible thing are we supposed to have done?"

"Let's not start the playing-innocent game. You know you disrupted an assembly."

"Disrupted?" Garcia replied. "We were part of an artistic performance."

"Oh, come on," said Crawley. "Cut it."

"Respectfully, sir," Garcia insisted. "We were all part of a theatrical event."

"Get real, pal," Crawley said.

"This was part of a time-honored theatrical tradition," Garcia explained. "We were breaking down the implied wall between the audience and the performers. The fourth wall, as scholars call it."

"You were inciting a riot," Crawley said.

"Some riot!" snorted Ippolito. "A riot of custard pies?"

"Lemon meringue," Sims corrected him.

"The point," said Crawley, "is that somebody could've gotten hurt."

"Yeah," said Schwarzkopf. "Us! We took those pies right in the schnoz."

"It's not as though we were firing a shotgun into the crowd or something," Daley said. "I mean, the only way we could have had a riot was if kids started jumping the stage to get their own hunks of pie."

"That's my point," said Crawley. The rest of us stared at the top of his head, where the point was, and tried not to giggle. "There's no telling what can happen when things get out of hand. That's why we have rules."

"Yes, but improvisation is at the very heart of the theater," Garcia intoned solemnly. "It's become extremely important to everyone who appears on stage."

"Fine," said Crawley, who clearly had no idea what Garcia was talking about. "Then you should have told the committee what you were planning to perform."

"But then the improvisation would have been lost," said Garcia more seriously than I would have thought possible under the circumstances. "All the spontaneity would have gone out of it—all the freshness."

Crawley let out a big sigh. If someone had told him he would have to spend his life dealing with Obnoxious Jerks and obnoxious jerks, he probably would have gone into some nice calm, relaxing profession such as air traffic controller or bomb detonator. "All right. The point isn't that this was mortally dangerous. The point is that you disrupted an assembly."

" 'Disrupted'?" Wu laughed. " 'Woke up' is more like it. Everybody was going to sleep in there before we did our thing."

Crawley shook his head and started over. "I don't really care about your opinion. In my opinion, and in the opinion of many of the teachers present, you disrupted a school assembly. You broke the rules. And school rules are designed to be—"

"Arbitrary," said Sims.

"Capricious," said The Schneid.

"Silly," said Daley.

"Broken," said Schwarzkopf.

Crawley was beginning to get angry. "I know that's what you think. But you guys are just a little too cute for your own good. Believe you me, you're going to have to work on that attitude if you expect a good college recommendation from this administration."

"Come on," said Daley. "We do our work. We get straight A's most of the time."

"Except in gym," said The Schneid.

"Right," Ippolito agreed. "Arborio wouldn't give one of us an A if we ran a three-minute mile."

Wu stared at Crawley. "What do you want from us anyway?"

"We want you to obey the rules. Is that so hard?"

"Not when the rules make sense," Schwarzkopf replied.

"Right," said Garcia. "You don't see us bringing guns or drugs to school. You don't see us beating up on kids in the hallways. There are lots of rules around here that we don't break."

"Believe me, I appreciate that," said Crawley. "But that's the whole point. You can't just obey the laws you think are fair. You have to obey all of them."

"I guess you never drove faster than the speed limit," said Ippolito.

"You guys." Crawley shook his head. He scribbled something on his official notepad. It was crystal clear he'd had enough of us for one day. "Two hours detention." He handed a piece of paper to me. "And another hour on Monday. Now get out of here."

We all cracked up when we got back out in the hall. We congratulated ourselves on our success with a lot of high fives. On the way over to detention we tossed a note in Demetrios's locker to warn him that today's official Obnoxious Jerks meeting had been postponed on account of Crawleyism.

We also told the pie brigade about Leslie's performance. They'd missed it, of course, since they were ushered out the doors of the auditorium and into Crawley's office right before Leslie went onstage.

As we went down the hall, we overheard this short, pimply freshman talking to his friend about how Donna Kerness had won the talent contest. Schwarzkopf couldn't believe it. He grabbed the freshman by the arm. "Tell us you're kidding. You must have her confused with someone else. You don't mean the girl who sang that folk song about stars and clouds, do you?"

The pimply kid nodded. "Yeah. That's the one. If you ask me, it should have been that girl who did the thing with the chewing gum."

Schwarzkopf kept shaking his head all the way down the hall. "Donna Kerness!" he muttered. "The judges must've thought it was supposed to be a contest to see who had the most guts getting up there on the stage."

The study hall became the detention hall after school. Today it was pretty empty. There were a couple of the kids you usually see in detention—the problem kids, kids with attitudes, kids who told their teachers exactly where to shove it. Smart kids were usually smart enough to know just how far they could bend the rules before they'd catch detention, so you didn't see smart kids there too often. Except sometimes after jerk-outs.

We all did the traditional thing of slamming our books on the table. It was just something you did. You took your backpack and really gave it a big old slam. It got out your frustrations, it got people's attention, and it made everybody think you were really angry at being stuck with detention even if you couldn't have cared less. Best of all, it annoyed whatever teacher was stuck running the detention hall that day.

"Hey, we're running a study hall here, not a boom box," said Mrs. Bresnahan, this tall, blond twelfth-grade history teacher who was probably the best-looking teacher in the school. Everybody figured with her looks, she must be dumb, but according to people's older brothers and sisters she was actually one of the smartest teachers in the school. Also one of the toughest graders. Anyway, that was the word on her from Perry Wu's older brother and a couple of other seniors we knew. We figured by the time we got to senior year, lucky Mr. Bresnahan would probably get transferred to some other city, and we'd be left with some horrendously ugly old ogre who graded on an easy curve. None of us thought that would be an improvement.

"Do any of you wonderful human beings have a note so I can find out why you're here and for how long?" Mrs. Bresnahan asked.

I made a face and got up to take her the note.

"So that was you guys with the pies," she said with a mild chuckle. "I guess you're here to grow up a little."

"Right," said Schwarzkopf. "Two hours' worth, anyway."

"And an hour on Monday," she reminded us. "You'd be surprised how much growing up you can do in that time."

"You don't say," said The Schneid.

"You guys act as though you invented the custard pie," said Mrs. Bresnahan.

"Lemon meringue," Sims corrected her.

"I've got news for you. Those pies were already stale back in the 1920s, in the silent-movie era."

"During your childhood, right?" Schwarzkopf asked.

"Very funny," said Mrs. Bresnahan. "You guys are real masters of comedy."

"If you really want to get technical about theater history," said Garcia, "you could claim custard pies were already stale two thousand years ago back in ancient Greece."

"Tasted pretty good for something that old," Schwarzkopf said. "Probably chock-full of weird Greek preservatives."

Garcia shot him a dirty look for interrupting. "After all, slapstick comedy goes back at least that far. So you could say it's been dead since before the birth of Christ. Or you could say it's something humans have enjoyed since then."

"In case you didn't notice," Ippolito pointed out for Mrs. Bresnahan's benefit, "we did get some laughs."

"I'll take your word for it," she said. "But the real question is whether people were laughing with you or at you. No answers necessary. Think about it, okay? Study time, everybody. The usual rules apply." The usual rules meant no talking, no passing notes, no games—that last one was apparently a leftover from the days when the school had a couple of chess whizzes—and at least one book open on your desk even if you weren't actually reading it.

There shouldn't have been anything awful about detention, really, since you could use the time to get some of your homework done, but it always seemed awful. It was in the ugliest room in the school, with not so much as a poster on the walls, and it was always a little too dark, and you felt like a prisoner who couldn't wait to get out. Which, of course, was the idea. I didn't spend much time in detention, but boy, did I ever hate it. On the other hand, it wasn't a whole lot different from study hall. Which I hated too. Somehow a classroom is okay when there's a teacher up there lecturing at you or you're taking a test and you at least have something to concentrate on or concentrate against. But there's something terrible about being stuck in a classroom with nothing to do but read one of your schoolbooks.

My strategy for surviving study hall was to work on math, because at least it kept you occupied. But now I'd already done my math in study hall, which left me a lot of reading in history and science and social studies and English. I generally enjoyed what we had to read in English, so I decided to save that work for home. I figured I'd get started on the chem homework since I still didn't understand Ms. Kurelek's explanation of Boyle's law. The Schneid had taken to calling it Cole's law, since it was about as tasty as the stuff you get on the side with your burger.

Anyway, I was buried in pressure and volume when the door opened. I looked up. So did the rest of us. It was Leslie. Schwarzkopf started clapping, and the rest of us joined in. Leslie gave us a nervous little nod of acknowledgment.

"Apparently you have a fan club," Ms. Bresnahan said. Leslie nodded uncomfortably and handed her the note. Mrs. Bresnahan unfolded it. "You too? I suspect this sets the single-assembly record for detentions. Have a seat. Usual rules."

Leslie walked to the very back of the room and dumped her stuff on the floor there. She was probably a first-timer when it came to detention. She didn't even slam her books down on the table.

"And the rest of you guys," said Mrs. Bresnahan, "can you manage to control your demonstrations until you get out of here?"

"She got gypped," said Schwarzkopf. "Conned. Screwed. She deserved the prize. No two ways about it."

I looked back. Leslie smiled a little.

"I'm sure Miss Freeze appreciates your support," said Mrs. Bresnahan. "Now, would you be kind enough to zip your lip?"

"I'm serious," Schwarzkopf went on. "I can't believe they actually gave the prize to Dorky Donna Kerness."

"The one who sang all those dumb folk songs?" said the mean-looking guy with the scruffy beard. "She won it?"

"Guys . . ." said Mrs. Bresnahan in frustration.

"She won it, all right," said Schwarzkopf. "I ask you."

"I ask you," said Mrs. Bresnahan. "Do you want to spend all next week here?"

"God, no," said Schwarzkopf.

"Then silence, please?"

"My lips are sealed," Schwarzkopf replied with his zipper gesture.

"Keep 'em that way," said Mrs. Bresnahan.

I looked back again. Leslie was nervously twirling a strand of hair around her little finger. Looking at her, it was hard to believe that she had wrapped a whole crowd of people around that finger less than an hour before. Now she was just another kid in detention.

Precisely one hour later she got up and left. "Have a good weekend," said Mrs. Bresnahan.

"Thanks," Leslie muttered shyly and headed out the door.

"She's in," I mumbled to Joe Ippolito. "Right?"

"Bring it up at next week's meeting," Ippolito mumbled back.

"What about this week's meeting?"

"In case you didn't notice, this week's meeting is right here in study hall."

"I hear mumbling," Mrs. Bresnahan said in a singsong voice without even looking up from her work.

Ippolito and I both went "Mumble, mumble, mumble" a little louder. Mrs. Bresnahan stared hard at us.

We shut up. As I said, smart kids generally know just how far you can go.

13

"Come on," I told Ippolito on the way home. "I can't believe you don't want her to join the Obnoxious Jerks."

"What are you saying? Does her personality magically change because she got up there on stage and did a good job?"

"It doesn't change," I said. "It just shows us what she's really like."

"Are you kidding? All it shows us is what she's like onstage. Offstage she's still this shy little mouselike thing."

"I thought you were the one who said Perry was like that until he joined."

"What I said was that we thought Perry was like that, and then we found out we were wrong, and then we asked him to join. Same as with you, only different. This group is delicate. We can't just invite the whole world in."

"Since when did Leslie Freeze become the whole world?"

"Don't I remember having this discussion before? I don't think we're ready to invite her yet."

"When do you think we will be?"

"When Leslie Freezes over hell."

"Nice pun. But seriously."

Ippolito sighed. "Look, I don't know."

"What if I bring her up at the meeting? Nominate her for membership?"

"I wish you wouldn't."

"Give me two good reasons."

"It'll make the meeting incredibly boring."

"That's not even one reason, let alone a good one."

"Okay. Here's a good one. You don't even know if she still wants to join."

That one stopped me for a minute. "You're right," I said. "So let's invite her to join, and if she says no, tough nuts. Weren't you the one who said that new members don't ask us, we ask new members?"

"I'm telling you, Back, we have a history to respect here. You're the new guy, and you come in with all guns blazing and want to change everything."

"I don't want to change anything. I just want to give Leslie a chance to join. I'm going to nominate her at the next meeting."

"Then you'll lose. We'll vote her down."

"What makes you so sure?"

"I don't think she's got the votes."

"There wasn't anybody in study hall who didn't applaud when she came in."

"That doesn't mean they're going to vote her into the Obnoxious Jerks. That doesn't mean she has what it takes."

"Oh, yeah? What does it take?"

"Guts," Ippolito said. "A sense of humor."

"And she didn't show guts with that performance of hers? She didn't show a sense of humor?"

"Different," said Ippolito.

"How is it different?" I demanded.

Ippolito stopped short right in front of me and turned very serious. "Look, I'm asking you as my personal best friend not to bring Leslie up at the next meeting."

"I just don't understand why not."

"Because if she gets in, things will change. The Obnoxious Jerks will change."

"We can't ever change? We're supposed to stagnate?"

"I'm telling you, things won't be the way they were. And we won't be able to put them back."

"In other words, because she's a girl."

Ippolito sighed. "Okay. Have it your way. Because she's a girl." He stared at me. "Did you ever hear of a group like ours—like the Lords—like fraternities and sororities—that was girls and boys together? Name one."

I thought. The only thing I could think of that came close was the Elks Club. My grandfather was a member. My grandmother was too, sort of, in what they called a ladies' auxiliary. But the ladies' auxiliary always had separate meetings from the men, so they weren't exactly full-fledged members. I shrugged and threw up my hands.

"See? There's something about it. I don't make the rules," Ippolito said.

"Wait a second. I thought we were supposed to be the ones who *fought* rules when they were stupid."

"Maybe this one isn't so stupid," Ippolito said.

I just shook my head and made a face.

Ippolito calmed down a little. "Look, all I'm asking you to do is hold on. Not rush into it. I still don't think we know her all that well. Think it over, okay?"

I said okay, I'd think it over. I was still thinking it over when I went through my front door. I was thinking it over when I went up to my room and changed into my jeans. I still had my mind on Leslie when I went into the dining room, where my little sister Jenny innocently asked me how the Obnoxious Jerks meeting was.

"Fine," I muttered into my salad.

"That's not what I heard," she declared in that incredibly irritating singsongy-snotty tone she used when she had just found out some piece of hot information from a friend of hers whose sister was in my grade. "I heard you had detention after school."

"What's this?" asked my father.

"I heard why too," Jenny announced.

"Maybe we should let Frank speak for himself instead of reporting gossip, Jenny," my mom scolded.

I didn't say anything, and neither did anybody else. "Well, speak, great brother," said my sister. "Speak."

"Do you mind?" I told her. "What I do is none of your damned business."

"Who says?" Jenny demanded.

"I say," I said.

"All right," my mom broke in. "Did you have detention or not, Frank?"

"Yeah," I muttered into my plate.

"You want to tell us about it?" my dad asked.

"Not particularly," I said.

"Tell us anyway," my dad said.

I took a bite of my salad.

"Frank . . ." said my mom.

"I know what happened," Jenny interrupted. "He and his Obnoxious Jerks were in the school talent show and they made fun of the school song and threw pies at each other. That's what happened."

"Thanks," I said.

"Is that what happened?" my father wanted to know.

"Pretty much. No big deal."

"Why do you keep asking for trouble?" my mother demanded. "You get good grades. You hang out with a

95

smart bunch of kids. So what's the problem? Don't you want to get good college recommendations? Don't you want to be more popular?"

"What? With the brain-dead? Everybody else in the school wants to be popular. We don't give a damn."

"That's obvious." Jenny laughed.

"Well, maybe you should," said Mom.

I glanced at my dad, who was chewing on his salad. "Maybe I've got something wrong," I said. "I thought the idea of school was supposed to be to learn, not to make you into some sort of toady like everybody else."

"When you get into the corporate world," Mom said, "you'll discover you have to go along with the rules."

"Well, maybe I won't get into the corporate world," I said. "Maybe I'll do something different."

"Garbageman," Jenny said.

"Why not?" I said. "Their business is always picking up."

Everybody at the table groaned. "That is so old, it has whiskers on it," Mom said.

"Its whiskers have whiskers," said Dad. "Look, you're not going into the corporate world tomorrow. But you are planning to go to college. You could use a decent recommendation. So in the meantime, try to stay out of detention. Okay?"

"It's not like we were trying for detention," I said. "That's just what happened."

"Okay?" my father repeated.

"Okay," I muttered.

"Pass the margarine," said my father. "Please."

After dinner I went up and flopped down on my bed and did some thinking. This business with Leslie was a problem, all right. On the one hand I thought she really deserved to be an Obnoxious Jerk. She was obviously smart enough, and she certainly proved she had our weird sense of humor.

On the other hand I understood what Ippolito meant about her being a girl. I mean, just going by my little sister, you could see girls and guys have different interests. Did I ever pay attention to the good-looking girls on the TV shows when I was her age? Well, yeah, sort of, but not to the point of buying magazines about them or plastering posters of them all over my walls. All right, so I did have a lot of posters of good-looking women for a while there.

But for all I knew, Leslie's bedroom might look pretty much like mine did now: one or two posters of good-looking women in bathing suits, a bunch of posters of bluegrass greats such as Bill Monroe and Lester Flatt and Earl Scruggs, and some souvenirs from places I'd lived, such as the New Jersey Devils pennant over my bed. Somehow I doubted it, though.

And I could see that if someone like Leslie joined the Obnoxious Jerks, it really might mean the group would change in some subtle way that was hard to describe. Maybe she'd be like Wrist Demetrios—afraid to go along with a lot of the fun. And somehow it would be hard for us to kid around about girls the way we often did.

But hey, we could do that kind of talking when she wasn't around. The real question as far as I was concerned—and really as far as everybody was concerned —was what Leslie would add to the Obnoxious Jerks. And that was the one that nobody could answer, since none of us knew her well enough. Because when you got right down to it, none of us knew any of the girls well enough.

The good-looking, attractive girls, the cheerleader types, wouldn't hang around with anybody less than a Lord. Which was fine with us, because the few times we attempted to have intelligent conversations with them, it was like trying to talk with aliens from the planet

Stupid. But most of the smarter girls in our class wanted to go out with the social-climbing Viscounts. As for the Obnoxious Jerks—well, let's put it this way: One reason that Leslie had become sort of an issue with the Obnoxious Jerks—or at least with Ippolito and me—was that she was the only girl in the sophomore class of Ullman Griswold Memorial High who had paid any Obnoxious Jerk the slightest bit of attention.

Ippolito was right: I *didn't* really know Leslie. I didn't know any more about her than the way she behaved in class and the fact that she had once been interested in joining the Obnoxious Jerks. I mean, I wouldn't have guessed in a million years that I'd see her doing the kind of act she did at the talent show.

So I decided I had to get to know her better. And I figured there was only one way to do it. I decided to ask her out.

There was one slight problem. I had never asked a girl out in my entire life.

14

I thought awhile about who you could ask for advice about asking a girl to go out with you. My parents? Their suggestions would probably be twenty-five years out of date. My sister? All she would do is laugh at me and make some snotty remark about how if I didn't know, she certainly couldn't tell me. Any of my fellow Obnoxious Jerks? Not likely. I couldn't remember one of them ever talking about going out with any girls.

The only person I could think of was my best friend back in Georgia, Harold Bergdahl. Harold had never been out with anybody when I knew him, but I had the feeling that had changed. Harold was tall and blond and so outrageously handsome you would actually see girls turn their heads when they went by. That didn't faze him much, because he happened to be real smart too— the smartest kid I'd ever met until I moved to Froston. He always said he couldn't stand hanging around with people who thought algebra was something a girl named Algie wore under her shirt.

So I picked up the phone and called Harold. I figured maybe my parents wouldn't notice when they got the phone bill, since they often made calls to their old friends in Georgia. If they did notice, I could always claim I was doing research for a school project, a paper on "My Best Friend" or something. And if they didn't believe that and made me pay—well, I'd just have to scrape up the ten dollars or whatever it cost one way or another.

Harold's mother answered. When I asked for Harold, she suspiciously wanted to know who was calling. When I told her, she turned supercheerful. "No kidding! Are you in town, Frank?" And when I told her no, she hollered at Harold to hurry up and pick up the phone, it was long distance.

"Hello?" Harold said.

"Hi," I said. "It's Frank."

"Frank! No kidding! How are you doing?"

"Okay," I said. "How about you?"

"All right. Listen, hang on a second. I want to take this upstairs. There are spies lurking down here."

"Okay." I heard his footsteps going upstairs.

"Frank? How are your parents?" Harold's mother inquired.

"Fine. Just fine."

"Do you like it up there where it's cold?"

"It's not so bad now. The winter was rough, though."

"Hang up, Mom," Harold said.

"Do I hear a 'please' in there?"

"Please," Harold said urgently.

"Give my regards to your folks," said Mrs. Bergdahl. "Bye, now."

"Bye," I said, and then her phone clicked off.

"You promised to write," Harold reminded me.

"Yeah, I know," I said sheepishly. "So did you."

"You promised first. Some friend. Not even a birthday card."

"I don't remember one from you, either."

"I may forgive you, but don't count on it. What's the deal?"

"Not much. School's okay, more or less. The winter was pretty horrible."

"Hey, we even had snow down here three or four times. I thought about you up there shoveling the walks and stuff."

"We actually bought an electric snowblower. Otherwise it's too hard to get out of the driveway when you get a big storm."

"Is it snowing right now?"

"Will you give me a break? It's May. It's getting downright warm."

"Listen, this must be costing you a fortune."

"Glad you noticed."

"What's the occasion?"

"I've got a minor problem."

Harold laughed. "You and everybody else on the planet."

"Seriously. I thought you could give me some advice."

"Speak to me."

"It's about this girl."

"Like I said: You and everybody else on the planet."

"Can I get three words in edgewise?"

"Not until you answer a couple of questions first. Is she pretty?"

I had to think about that one. "I mean, she's not Miss America."

"Then she must be smart."

"Yeah. She's smart."

"Okay. I just didn't want you to waste your time on some gorgeous airbrain."

"Harold, you forget. The gorgeous airbrains wouldn't waste their time on me. You, yes. Me, no."

"So what's the problem?"

"I want to ask her out."

"I repeat: What's the problem?"

"Well, I'm not sure how to do it."

"You ask her to go out with you. What's the big deal?"

"I've never done this before, that's the big deal."

"Aha! The truth will out. Just do it, that's all. Ask her out."

"Where do I ask her to go? Do I ask her over the phone or what? What if she says no? I don't know this stuff."

"What are you trying to do? Impress her?"

"I don't care if I impress her or not. I just want to talk to her. Find out more about her."

"Okay. So you want to go somewhere where you can talk. That leaves out the movies. Go to a museum or a zoo or the park or something. Somewhere you can spend time together."

I hadn't thought of that. "All right. Let's say it's the zoo."

"Fine. Zoos are very romantic."

"Maybe I should pick someplace else."

"You don't feel romantic about this girl you want to go out with?"

"Not particularly."

"You're not serious."

"Look, all I want to do is talk to her for a while. Find out more about her."

"Why?"

I sighed. "It's kind of complicated."

"All right. Let's stick with the zoo. Now, how do you get there?"

"That's a good question." I snorted.

"You're still not driving, right?"

"August twenty-third, remember? I'm counting the days."

"You can't believe how neat it is."

"I can believe it, all right. But it's not going to do me any good as far as this date is concerned."

"Is there a bus you can take?"

"Yeah, I guess. I'll have to check the schedule."

"Okay. Find out. Then remember, you have to offer to pay. Take enough money to pay for her bus fare. Also her lunch. Birdseed. Bear food. Stuff like that."

"I thought women's lib took care of stuff like that."

"Right, *if* she refuses to let you pay. But believe me, she won't. They never do."

"What else?" I asked.

"What else is there? All you have to do is call her up and say you were wondering if she'd like to go to the zoo with you whenever it is you want to go. That's not so hard, is it?"

"Doesn't sound like it," I admitted. "Provided she says okay."

"She will. If she says she's busy, ask her if there's another time that'd be better for her. If she says yes, make a new plan. If she says no, forget about her. She's not interested, and that's that."

"Well, that sounds simple enough."

"Hundreds of thousands of morons do it every day. You should be able to manage."

I felt superrelieved. And kind of stupid. Of course it was easy. I should have known it all along. "Man, I knew you'd know. I just knew it. Thanks."

"Go to it, son. And good luck."

"Hey, it's great to talk to you again. Any chance you're going to visit up north?"

"About as likely as snow on the Fourth of July. How

103

about you? Your parents thinking about coming back for a visit?"

"About as likely as snow on Labor Day. How about writing?"

"Don't make promises you can't keep."

"I didn't make any promises. I said maybe."

"Well, you know where I am. Least you could do is let me know how you make out with the lady."

"How's your love life?"

"Airbrains," he said, and I could almost see him shaking his head. "Nothing but airbrains." Gorgeous girls were probably hanging off his shoulders every time he went to school.

"See you," I said.

"Not if I see you first," said Harold Bergdahl. He would have made a perfect Obnoxious Jerk.

I hung up the phone. Good old Harold! I knew I could count on him! I reached for the phone book on the little shelf on the phone stand.

I picked up the phone again. I dialed Leslie's number. I heard the ringing on the other end.

Whatever Leslie had must have been contagious. All of a sudden *I* felt like throwing up.

My stomach felt as though it had moved up around my throat. What I really wanted to do was slam the phone down and give up this crazy idea of asking Leslie to go out with me. I mean, Harold had made it sound easy, but now it didn't seem easy at all. Besides, I didn't owe Leslie anything. Why should I care whether she joined the Obnoxious Jerks?

Right. So instead of hanging up the phone when Leslie's mom said "Hello?" how come I made this kind of strangled sound?

"Hello?" Leslie's mom said again. See? It *wasn't* easy. Harold hadn't said a word about what to do if her mother answered.

"Is Leslie there?" I managed to squeak out.

"Yes," she said cheerfully. "Who's calling?"

Harold hadn't said anything about what to do if her mother asked who I was, either. "Frank," I said. "Frank Wess."

"One minute," she said.

It was a long minute. I could hear her shout, "It's for you!" and Leslie shout back, "Who is it?" and her mom shout back, "Somebody named Frank Wess," and Leslie say what sounded like "Oh, God!" and shout, "I'll take it upstairs!"

I don't know why this seemed so difficult—I mean, I never had this problem when I phoned my friends and their parents answered—but I kept thinking I should slam the phone down and end this right now. Except now Leslie knew it was me on the phone.

"Hello?" she said in that nervous voice of hers.

"Hi," I said.

"Frank?" she said.

"Yeah," I said.

"How are you?" she said.

"Okay," I said.

"How long did they keep you in detention?"

"Two hours. And then we have to do another hour on Monday."

"God! I guess I got off easy."

"Well, all you did was crack everybody up and insult teachers. You didn't incite a riot."

"Yeah, I guess."

"It really was a great routine. Everybody said so."

"Thanks. I tried."

We were getting nowhere fast. "Uh . . . what I wanted to say was I was, uh, wondering, uh . . . if you'd like to go out and do something."

"Go out and do something?"

"Maybe tomorrow?"

"Tomorrow?"

"I thought maybe the zoo?" I said.

"The zoo?" she replied with what sounded like a slightly sarcastic giggle.

"I've never been there since I moved here. I thought it might be good for a few laughs."

"The zoo," she said again, this time more thoughtfully. "Yeah, okay. What time?"

We worked it out. I was supposed to stop by her place at noon. We were going to have lunch at the zoo. Harold was sort of right after all: Once we got over the initial hump, it wasn't too hard really. She didn't exactly sound overjoyed about the whole thing, but at least she didn't act as though it was the worst idea she'd ever heard.

Everything went okay until I thought we had settled pretty much everything. Then she said, "I just have one more question, Frank. Why are you doing this?"

"Doing what?"

"Asking me out like this. I mean, just calling me up like this, out of the blue."

"I don't know," I said. "I thought it would be fun."

"Okay," she said, sounding as though she was in a big hurry to get off the phone. "See you tomorrow." She hung up.

Well, I'd done it. Now all I had to do was manage not to screw it up somehow. I used to have a lot of fun at zoos when my parents had taken me to them when I was a kid. Feed the bears, make faces at the monkeys, all that stuff. Thank you, Harold Bergdahl.

Ten seconds later the phone rang. I was sure it was Leslie calling back to tell me she'd changed her mind. I hesitated a second before I picked it up and nervously said hello.

It was Ippolito. "You sound weird," he said. "What's shakin'?"

"Not a whole lot." For about half a second I wondered whether to tell him about my date, or whatever it was, with Leslie. Then I decided not to. For some reason I decided it wasn't any of his business.

"We rescheduled the meeting," he said. "On account of the unforeseen cancellation."

"For when?" The second I finished saying it, I knew the answer as positively as if I had ESP.

"Tomorrow. One o'clock. We're planning the first big softball game of the year."

"I thought Sims had ballet lessons Saturday afternoons."

"His ballet teacher's sick," Ippolito informed me.

"Wonderful," I said, shuddering at the thought of phoning Leslie back and changing everything. "But I've already got plans for tomorrow."

"What kind of plans?" Ippolito asked.

I couldn't explain it, but the more I talked with Ippolito, the less I wanted to tell him about Leslie and me. I mean, he was only my best friend, that was all, but somehow I didn't want him to know about this. In a crazy way I felt kind of embarrassed about it. "I've just got a bunch of stuff to do."

"So do it on Sunday," Ippolito said. "You don't want to miss the meeting."

"I don't want to miss the meeting. But I'm going to have to. I've just got other plans."

"What are these top-secret plans of yours that are so important they can't be changed?" Ippolito demanded.

I stalled.

"What?" Ippolito pressed. "You're not going to another one of those Lords meetings, are you?"

This was kind of a running gag that came up every so often when somebody really wanted to irritate me. Way back at the very beginning of the school year when I didn't know better, I had actually gone to a meeting of the Lords because this guy across the street invited me. It had been one of the very worst experiences of my life.

"Get serious," I said. "I just can't come to the meeting, is all. It's no big deal. I'll be there next Friday."

"Suit yourself," said Ippolito. "Doesn't matter to me one way or the other. But if you want to behave like some character in a spy novel, your mysterious ways are going to be the number one topic of conversation at the meeting."

"Let them. I don't care."

"What about the movie tomorrow night? Are we still on for that, or has your incredibly important engagement screwed that up too?"

I had forgotten about that. But I figured I could get done at the zoo in plenty of time. "We're still on for the movie."

"Well, thanks a whole bunch for keeping your appointments!" Ippolito said sarcastically.

"You don't have to get repulsive. It's not as though this Jerks meeting was scheduled months in advance."

"Twenty-seven cents. Plus tax!"

I'd committed the one Obnoxious Jerks sin. "You got me irritated."

"No excuse. Jerks and Obnoxious Jerks are in no way the same. The fine will help you remember."

"Okay, okay," I said irritably. "Twenty-seven cents plus tax. Fine."

"And the problem isn't that you're not showing up. It's that you're being so damned secretive about it. Just remember: No mysteries are safe from the all-seeing, all-knowing eyes of the Obnoxious Jerks."

"Yeah, right. I'll remember."

"Anyhow, at least there's one thing good about this," Ippolito remarked.

"What's that?"

"We're not going to have to waste valuable softball time in a knock-down, drag-out battle over making that Iceberg friend of yours a member."

16

I had no idea why my brain and my stomach insisted on making such a big deal about all this. It wasn't really a date or anything. Leslie and I were just going to spend the afternoon together at the zoo. Nothing earth-shattering about that.

Yet I was unwilling to breathe a word about it even to my best friend. So the last thing I needed was to run into one of my fellow Obnoxious Jerks and have him ask why I wasn't going to the meeting and where I was going instead. I actually planned my route over to Leslie's so that I'd slink around the back streets and avoid my friends. Getting a ride would have made things easier, but I didn't really feel like having my parents give me the third degree about this either.

I took a big loop around every street where I knew other Obnoxious Jerks lived, and I steered way clear of the little shopping street in our neighborhood where you always seemed to run into people you knew. So naturally, somewhere near Leslie's, on a street I'd never even been on before, I heard somebody hollering my name.

I didn't answer. I figured the best thing to do was pretend not to hear. Somebody either was hollering at some other Frank, in which case it didn't matter, or at me, in which case maybe whoever it was might go away. But then I heard "Frank! Hey, Frank! Wess!" louder. I suddenly realized it probably wasn't any of the Obnoxious Jerks, because they'd have yelled "Back!"

So I turned around. George Alton was rushing toward me on his bike. I felt incredibly relieved. At least he wasn't an Obnoxious Jerk.

He was still a plain old regular jerk, though. He jumped the curb and squealed to a stop about two inches in front of my toes. And that was only because I jumped away in the nick of time.

"Wess, do you have hearing difficulties?" he asked in the exact same tone of voice Coach Arborio would have used. George was probably a member of Future Gym Coaches of America.

"Yeah," I said. "I have trouble hearing people who try to run me over."

"I wouldn't run you over. Wouldn't want to mess up the bike. Scared you, though."

"All right. I was scared. I admit it. You're a regular Frankenstein." I stepped forward again, but he turned his bike wheel to block my way.

"Do you mind?" I said.

"Wess, why do you hang out with that bunch of losers?"

"You must be mistaking me for somebody else. I never hang out with the Lords."

"Very funny. You know what I'm talking about."

"I never know what you're talking about, because

you never make any sense. Now, do you mind if I get where I'm going?"

I tried to dodge past, but he blocked my way again. "You know something?" he said. "You guys are incredibly juvenile."

"Yeah," I said. "We're regular juvenile delinquents."

"That stunt with the pies yesterday? Real kid stuff. Sixth grade. Why don't you guys grow up?"

"Right. And be like you. Walk around sucking up to the administration, act like we're the hottest things on three legs, avoid the use of our brains, and pick on kids we don't like?"

"You know who's going to get the good college recommendations? The ones that say 'This fellow is a fine gentleman and a member of five extracurricular associations'?"

"Sure, I know. I also know who's gonna need them desperately when the College Board scores come down."

"For kids who are supposed to be the smartest in the school, you don't know doodly-squat. Is there even one girl in the entire school who will pay you the slightest bit of attention?"

"Is there even one girl who the Lords hang out with whose IQ is bigger than her bra size?" I'd had enough. I pushed past him, but he decided to ride alongside me.

"Grow up," Alton said.

I was getting close to Leslie's place by now. I really wanted to get rid of this moron. "You know what your problem is, George?"

"I'd love to hear," Alton said sarcastically.

"No imagination. The only thing you and your friends can think of is the same old stuff. The same music. The same beer. You can't stand for people to be different."

"And you know the problem with you and your friends? You act like jerks just to show off."

"We also act like jerks to prove we're not among the brain-dead like you."

"You really are jerks," Alton said. "You're missing all the fun."

"Like what? Getting drunk and puking all over your friends?"

"I'm telling you," Alton said smugly. "You're blowing the best years of your life."

I stopped short. "See?" I said. "There's the difference between you and me. If high school ends up being the best years of my life, then you can bet I screwed up somewhere. I want to get the hell out of high school and go finish college and run my own life. If these are the best years of your life, you're not just brain-dead now— you're totally dead the day you graduate."

Whew! I don't usually give speeches like that, but I knew exactly where this one came from—a conversation Ippolito and I were having after his older brother gave him some hassle about hanging out with the Obnoxious Jerks.

Of course it sailed right over George's thick head. "You guys are just too much," he snorted. Then he jumped the curb again, ran the bike about one inch from my toes, and took off down the street. I was so glad to see him go I didn't even shout at him.

Especially since I was homing in on Leslie's place and I was feeling kind of weird again. I saw the sign for her street, and I checked my pocket for the slip of paper with her address on it. Her house was just down the block and pretty much like ours—split-level, big front lawn, the usual suburban thing. I checked the number on the mailbox against the slip of paper one last time just to be absolutely sure. Then I took a deep breath, went up to the front door, and rang the bell. The door-bell must have been one of those electronic models you can program to play just about anything; what it played was the first few notes of "Girls Just Want to Have Fun." Nobody answered, so I pressed it again.

"One second!" I heard Leslie holler from inside. All of a sudden I got this choky strangled feeling in my throat again. It got chokier as I heard footsteps behind the door and somebody fiddling with the lock.

"Hi," Leslie said. She looked a whole lot different from the way she usually did in school. She was wearing a pair of black jeans and a T-shirt with some odd bright squiggly pattern on the front. She also seemed to be wearing some kind of purplish lipstick. She didn't look beautiful or anything, but she looked kind of—I didn't know—fun.

"Hi," I said. "You ready to go?"

"Yeah. I just have to get my purse. Want to come in a second?"

"Sure." I walked into the hallway. There were a couple of weird masks on the wall, humanlike forms but with long tusks and huge bug eyes and weird colors with stripes all over. They were kind of scary and hilarious at the same time. "What are those?" I asked.

"Javanese masks. They use them in some sort of ceremonies, but I'm not exactly sure what."

"Japanese?" I said, thinking I hadn't heard right.

"Javanese. From Java. One of those islands in the Pacific?"

"Oh, like Borneo."

"Right," Leslie said. "Yum, yum . . ."

". . . eat 'em up," we both said together. Then we gave each other these amazed looks.

"How'd you know about that?" I said.

"The Wild Man of Borneo? How'd *you* know about it?"

"I was really into the Little Rascals for a while.

114

When we lived down South, there was a station on cable that used to have it on early Sunday mornings before the cartoons."

"It used to be on here too," Leslie said. "I wish I'd taped 'em. The crazy thing is, I can't remember a single thing about that Wild Man episode except that line: 'Yum, yum, eat 'em up.' I think maybe Alfalfa sang in that one too."

"Remember the fat kid? What was his name?"

"Spanky McFarland. And Buckwheat, the black kid. And remember the dog with the black eye? What was his name?"

I couldn't remember. "Sparky?"

"That doesn't sound right."

"Dude," I said. "Spud. Fred the Dog."

Leslie made a face. "Really."

"All right. So we forgot the dog's name."

Leslie looked thoughtful. "I know that name. It'll come to me. I'm sure of it." She looked in her purse and took out her keys. "You ready to go?"

"Sure."

We walked out the door. "I can remember exactly what that dog looked like, with the eyepatch and everything," Leslie said as she locked up.

"Me too," I said. "Patchface? Midnight? Blackie?"

She shook her head. "We'll get it. You wait. God, remember. Now I know what old people feel like." And all of a sudden she turned her face all puckery and wizened and her voice got totally creaky, kind of like when the wicked witch in *Snow White* turns into the old hag. "Heh, heh, heh," Leslie said. "I just can't seem to remem . . . remem . . . what was I saying?"

Just as suddenly she changed back into her normal self and said, "Well, anyway . . ." Except by now I was beginning to wonder what her normal self really was.

Was it the quiet, mousy Leslie we saw in class every day, or the sarcastic, superconfident Leslie from the stage, or somebody in between?

Everything was cool on the way to the bus stop. I had been wondering what we'd talk about, but we had a lot of school stuff in common—this and that about French class and La Feldstein, and different kinds of interesting gossip about other teachers and so on. Then George turned up again.

Lord Alton pulled up in front of us and mumbled snottily, "Well, *her* IQ is bigger than her bra size." Leslie, as I probably mentioned, is ultraskinny. But before I had a chance to snap anything back, he was down over the handlebars and racing away. I was going to shout a couple of choice obscenities at him and give him the finger, but with Leslie there I couldn't bring myself to do it.

"What was that all about?" Leslie asked, half embarrassed and half furious.

"Our Lord and—he thinks—master. He ran into me on the way over to your place. We had a high-level intellectual discussion," I said sarcastically.

"I'll bet. Was that crack about me?"

It was kind of embarrassing. I stammered a little before I said, "Actually you should be flattered. I told George the Lords never hang out with women whose IQ is bigger than their bra size."

"Funny line." Leslie shook her head and scowled. "Yeah, real flattering, all right. My IQ could be thirty-three. My mother says there's nothing wrong with being flat, but I notice she doesn't have that problem."

"You look fine," I said.

"Thanks for the support—as Monica Cartwright told her bra." Monica Cartwright was famous for having the biggest breasts of anyone at UGH. "I don't have a whole lot of choice about it, do I?"

"Why do women think all that guys are interested in are their breasts?"

"Probably because that's all guys really are interested in. Except you, of course. I still can't figure out why you asked me to do this thing with the zoo today."

"I don't know. Why'd you pick me to ask about joining the Obnoxious Jerks?"

"Because I thought you'd understand."

"Well, I did. I told you. I tried."

"I was wondering whether I could sue you guys for sex discrimination."

"Sex discrimination?"

"Yeah. You have an organization that deliberately discriminates against and excludes women."

"I don't know. First of all, we aren't exactly what anybody would call organized. And second of all, we don't have any rule that says girls can't join."

"No? I thought you did."

"Not really. But then we don't have official rules about much of anything, except corn chips and stuff."

"Well, how many members do you have?"

I counted in my head. "Eight. No, nine."

"And how many of those are women?"

"Zero. Zip."

"*De facto* evidence of discrimination."

"De facto?" Leslie really knew some good terms.

"Meaning just that fact alone indicates you're discriminating."

"We probably are," I admitted. "But then so are the Lords and all the other groups in the school."

"Oh, great! So you're saying you model the Obnoxious Jerks after the Lords?"

"That's the last thing we'd ever do. You aren't really going to sue us, are you?"

"I checked with my mother. She's a lawyer. Turns

out I can't. Not unless you're using public facilities or doing business at your meetings."

"You still want to join?"

"You don't think I'd be an asset to the group?"

"Hey, I'm all for it, mostly. It's the other guys you have to convince."

"Mostly?"

At that point I went into some of the philosophical points Ippolito had raised, without mentioning him of course. But we had reached the bus stop, and there was a bus waiting, and that changed the subject. I felt incredibly relieved. I was sure I'd run into some Obnoxious Jerks at the bus stop, but now my secret was still safe.

When we got on the bus, Leslie paid for herself before I got a chance to mention anything about it. I figured the best thing to do was let it go by. I figured that's what Harold Bergdahl would have done.

We found seats together near the back. Leslie nudged me and pointed up ahead. There was a guy eating peanuts out of a jar way up front. He was tossing them in the air and catching them in his mouth. He didn't miss too often, but when he did and a peanut bounced off his nose into one of his neighbors, people gave him dirty looks. Leslie started imitating him, catching imaginary peanuts in her mouth or missing them and bouncing them off her nose. I started to laugh, but Leslie pretended I was being rude and hushed me up. Then she "missed" one so obviously I could almost feel it hit me, and I pretended to be indignant as I "brushed" it off.

"Sorry," Leslie said. "I missed."

"You'd better not do that again, young lady," I said. We both cracked up. A couple of people actually gave us dirty looks.

"You're really good at this stuff," I said. "Are you in the Drama Club?"

Her face clouded over. "Don't ask about that."

"Why not?"

Leslie sighed. "It's a long story."

I had a feeling I knew how to make it shorter. "The Lords?"

Leslie nodded. "And the Viscounts. And their girlfriends."

"What, they kept you out?"

"Yeah. They have tryouts. They pick their friends. Which is one reason the plays are so lousy every year."

"How come they let you into the talent show?"

"I'm still trying to figure that one out," Leslie said. "How come they let you in?"

"We did a great act. Not the one we did onstage."

"Same here. I mean, considering how close to the bottom of the barrel they scraped to get some of those acts, maybe they decided they *had* to take us."

"Do you take acting classes?"

"Yeah. That's why I was almost late when you came over. I just got back from one this morning."

"Man, you were good yesterday. Really good."

"Oh, yeah, right. So good I lost my cookies."

"I just thought you were commenting on *our* act," I said.

Leslie let out a laugh so loud everybody on the bus turned around to stare at us.

We got out at the zoo, but Leslie refused to let me pay her way there, either. She said it was the kind of thing Lords would do for their women. She wouldn't let me pay for her lunch either, even though she only had a vanilla yogurt. No wonder she was so skinny. If you have to pay, vegetarians make cheap dates. Personally, I had a burger with fries and a Coke and an ice cream cone. I was waiting for Leslie to make some remark about eating meat, but she didn't.

Then we hit the animals. Leslie knew where everything was. It turned out that she came to the zoo a lot. She liked to study the movements of the animals and mimic them. Her acting teacher had told her it was a great way to learn body control.

So we'd watch the bears, and Leslie would lumber around like one for a while. Then we'd check out the deer, and Leslie would act all skittish, making these tiny little frightened moves and leaps. She was really great as a monkey. She could halfway make you believe she was climbing trees and jumping from limb to limb.

I made a couple of feeble attempts at imitating the animals, but when I did it, I just looked stupid. Leslie really knew what she was doing. She also knew other things—such as which animals lived where and which ones were on the endangered species lists. It turned out she was a real zoo freak.

The afternoon really flew by. We saw everything in the zoo, and we must have imitated half of it. It was a terrific afternoon. On the bus home Leslie said, "I'm really glad you asked me to do this."

"I had a great time," I said.

"See? I was right about you Obnoxious Jerks."

"What do you mean?"

"Most interesting guys in the school?"

"Thanks," I said. "I guess."

"What do you mean, you guess?"

"I mean, I thought I was personally interesting, not just because I'm an Obnoxious Jerk."

"You are." Leslie flashed me a big smile.

Back at her place, we stood there in front of the door while she fumbled with her keys. Then she kissed me on the cheek, said, "Bye," and ran inside.

I stood there for a second, wondering whether I had lipstick on my face. I raised my hand to rub it off, and then I realized Leslie might be watching. I dropped my hand awkwardly to my side and walked around the corner. Then I pulled out some tissues and wiped my cheek. The tissues turned purplish.

You can bet I got rid of them before I got home. And you can also bet I scrubbed my face before I went down for dinner that night. Harold Bergdahl may have been right about some things being easier than they seem, but handling nosy parents and sisters definitely isn't one of them.

17

"Hey! Deserter! AWOL!" Ippolito shouted out the window of Demetrios's dad's car as it drove up to my place about six o'clock.

"What, I need official leave to attend to my own personal business?" I said as I got into the backseat.

"Right. It's in the Obnoxious Jerks constitution," said Demetrios.

The joke was that there was no Obnoxious Jerks constitution, but I didn't joke back. I still wasn't sure why, but I wanted to keep my afternoon with Leslie my own business.

Demetrios pulled out without looking, and a car behind us screeched to a halt. The rest of us shook our heads and made faces at each other. Demetrios was the first one of us to get his learner's permit, and he'd just gotten his junior license a couple of weeks ago. Knowing how weird his dad was about a lot of things, we were all pretty surprised that he'd let Wrist take the car out alone. Especially after we took our first ride with him. Demetrios seemed to think watching where he was going was sort of an option—nice once in a while, but not really essential.

"So what happened at the meeting?" I asked as I fastened my seat belt.

"Our lips are sealed," said Demetrios.

"Would you give me a break?" I said.

"First we want to know what you were doing that was so important you had to miss the meeting," Daley said.

"That," I replied wittily, "is for me to know and you to find out."

"What an original turn of phrase!" Ippolito said. "Did you make that up just now?"

"Come on, lay off. What's everybody so hot to know my business for?"

"If you must know, we're nosy," said Demetrios, turning around to look at me.

"Watch where you're going," Daley and I said at the same time.

"No backseat driving till you get your licenses," Demetrios replied.

"Look out!" Ippolito shouted. Demetrios turned frontwise again just in time to stop short of a parked truck up ahead. Daley looked at me, shook his head, and mouthed the word "scary."

Ippolito turned toward me as the car started rolling again. "You give us your facts, and we'll give you ours."

"This sounds like something the Lords would pull," I said. "We don't have any rules about attending meetings or anything like that. So lay off, okay?"

"Suit yourself," said Daley. "We'll find out one way or the other."

"Maybe," I said, thinking it was about time to change the subject. "Did you guys decide on a movie?"

"A nice attempt to change the subject," said Ippolito. "Fear not, the original topic shall return. The answer is yes: *Time to Kill.*"

"Some so-called thriller," Daley said.

"I offered to split a video rental," said Demetrios, "but Ippolito's really hot to see this thing."

"Not hot enough to guarantee our five bucks though," Daley pointed out.

"If you don't like it," said Ippolito, "I will personally give each of you a shiny engraved portrait of Abraham Lincoln."

"With the Lincoln Memorial on the back," I said.

"Which is probably just about what this flick will be worth," said Daley. "Hey, Wrist, look out!"

Demetrios nearly ran a red light. There was a cop sitting at the corner, and he gave us a dirty look as we screeched to a stop.

Somehow we got to the mall in one piece. I think it had something to do with other drivers getting out of our way. We razzed Demetrios about it all the way through the parking lot. He said we were just jealous and he couldn't wait till the rest of us got our licenses and screwed up.

One good thing about the mall is the Food Court, where you can get everything from enchiladas to chop suey. The bad thing is that a lot of the food really stinks.

"Sushi, anybody?" said Planet Daley.

Demetrios made a face. "Raw fish?"

"Hey, it's not so bad," Daley said. "Kind of fresh-tasting."

"I hate to bring you down," Ippolito said, "but you know my dad's a doctor. And he refuses to let me eat that stuff."

"Why's that?" Daley inquired.

"Because raw fish can have these amazingly disgusting parasites. Like liver flukes. They're kind of like tapeworms, except they live in your liver."

"Gross," said Demetrios.

"Hey, that's not the gross part," Ippolito said. "The gross part is that their eggs can get into your bloodstream and get caught in your tiniest blood vessels, your capillaries—such as the ones in your eye, which are especially narrow. Then when the eggs hatch, they can eat away at your eyeball from the inside."

"You're making that up," Demetrios said. "Or stole it from some dumb horror flick."

"Cross my heart," Ippolito replied. "Ask my dad next time you come over."

"Okay. No sushi here," I said.

"I'm not even sure I'm hungry anymore," said Planet Daley.

"Fine," said Ippolito. "You're elected to stand watch over a table while the rest of us hunt up food."

"Aw, come on," Daley said.

"Somebody has to do it," Ippolito said. "It's crowded in here."

Daley sighed. "All right. But hurry up." The rest of us went off in search of dinner.

When I got back to the table, Ippolito was eating the first part of his Taco Trio. Demetrios had some kind of lasagna. I put down the gyro sandwich I'd gotten from the Greek place. Daley headed for the Chinese stand.

"You realize," said Ippolito, "that no self-respecting Italian would be caught dead eating lasagna that looked like that."

Demetrios shrugged. "No self-respecting Greek would eat that gyro thing, either. Or your taco, for that matter."

"I have no comment unless Daley comes back with bratwurst," I said.

Daley came back with a plateful of glop that was

supposedly Chinese. "Perry Wu should be here to tell you what a load of crap that is," Ippolito said.

"I look at it this way," Daley said. "Anything's better than eating what my mom decides to thaw out in the microwave."

"Cafeteria food?" Demetrios inquired.

"Correction: almost anything," said Daley through a mouthful of his slop suey.

We ate awhile. I decided I might find out more about the meeting now that everybody had a full stomach. "Anybody want to tell me what happened this afternoon?"

"You tell us," Demetrios shot back with a strand of mozzarella hanging from his mouth.

"Hey, I'm a member," I reminded him. "I have a right to know what goes on at the meetings."

"Sure," Ippolito said. "All you have to do is show up."

"Come on," I complained. I was really beginning to get fed up with this crap.

"Come on yourself," said Daley. "We just want to know where you were this afternoon."

I could have told them. What the hell. But there was some kind of principle at stake here. "Forget it," I said, and bit into my gyro.

"What's the big deal? Why can't you tell us where you were?" Demetrios demanded.

"Look," I said, "the rest of us went to bat for you when you chickened out on the T-shirt thing. Nobody said anything. It was your decision, right?"

Demetrios looked kind of sheepish.

"And you helped out with the big pie thing yesterday, but nobody told Crawley you were involved, did they?"

Demetrios looked even more sheepish.

"So I mean, if the other guys want to be stupid and get on my back, at least you don't have to go along with them, do you, Wrist? And I'm damned angry at you too, Joe—and you, Planet."

Ippolito and Daley didn't say anything.

"I mean, what if I didn't go to the meeting because I had to go to the doctor because I had some embarrassing disease or something? Which is not what happened, by the way. But what if?"

"We'd want to know about it," said Daley.

"Yeah, but maybe I wouldn't want you to know about it," I said. "Some things aren't everybody else's business. So lay off, okay? If you don't want to tell me what happened at the meeting today, which is my business, since I'm a member in good standing, okay, fine. I'll find out from somebody else. But I'm not going to take any more of this hassle." I took a big bite out of my sandwich for emphasis.

"We finally elected an Official Snack Cake," said Demetrios in a slightly grudging tone.

"Devil Dogs?" I asked.

"Hostess Snowballs," said Daley. "What turned the tide was when The Schneid said it was the closest thing to a breast we're likely to bite into for a while."

"Nice going," I said. "Anything else happen?"

"Not much," Demetrios said. "If you've got a great idea for the next jerk-out, we'd sure like to hear it. Nobody else came up with one."

"Temporary," said Daley. "Purely a temporary state of affairs. We're still coasting on yesterday's triumph, that's all. But we can't get complacent. That's why the great teams don't repeat."

"Thank you, Wally Zengerman," said Demetrios.

Daley chopped the air with his right hand just the way Wally Zengerman, our local sportscaster, would. Everybody but Joe cracked up. For some reason Ippolito was in a sullen mood, not saying anything. The rest of us just ignored it.

"How'd the game go?" I asked.

"In about the second inning Sims tore the cover off the ball," Demetrios said. "Literally."

"You should've seen it. That thing went a mile," Daley marveled. "We had to send out an expeditionary force to buy a new one."

It sounded pretty much like any Obnoxious Jerks meeting. It would have been fun to be there.

"Damn!" Ippolito said. He had just taken a bite out of his third taco, and the innards somehow shot all over his shirt. The rest of us cracked up again.

"Yeah. Very funny," Ippolito said.

"It looks like you were mauled by some kind of frijole monster," I said.

"Yeah, right," Ippolito said, giving me a dirty look.

"It's *The Devil Taco*," Demetrios said, sounding like an ad for some bad horror flick. "Hot sauce from hell inflames it to a fever pitch."

Ippolito stood up, still staring at the spreading hot-sauce stain on his shirt.

"Where you going?" I asked.

"Hey, that's my line, isn't it?" he snarled at me. He turned to Demetrios and Daley and said, "I'm going to find some water and see if I can get this off. Back in a minute." He disappeared.

"What's with him tonight?" I asked Demetrios and Daley.

"What are you asking us for?" said Demetrios. "You're the ones who are supposed to be such good friends."

"He's being real pissy," I pointed out. "He wouldn't even say a word when you guys told me what happened at the meeting. I just thought maybe you knew why he's in this mood."

"I can tell you why," said Daley. "He's mad at you for keeping secrets from him."

"Secrets?" I asked.

"You know. Where you went this afternoon."

I sighed. "I wish everybody would get off my back about that. What if I told you I just stayed home and did some homework?"

"You didn't. Joe phoned your place right before the meeting. Your mom said you weren't home."

"Okay. So I wasn't home. We've been through this already. I mean, where does everybody think I was?"

"Hey, man, we don't really care where you were," said Daley. "You're right. It's Joe who's got the problem about this."

"Why should he care? Where does he think I was?"

"I know where he thinks you were," said Demetrios.

"Okay. I give up," I said. "Where?"

"He thinks you were hanging out with Leslie Freeze."

I didn't say anything. I just sat there. I wanted to put something in my mouth and pretend I was choking to cover up the shades of red and purple I knew I must be turning. But I'd already finished my sandwich, and the only other food on the table was Ippolito's shattered taco.

"Well? Were you?" asked Demetrios.

I somehow forced out the words. "Was I what?"

"Chilling out with Freeze," said Daley.

Ippolito returned. He had overheard enough to know what was going on. "That is what you were doing, right?"

"What if I was?" I said. "Is that—"

"Okay, so you were," Ippolito interrupted. "That's all I wanted to know."

"Speak for yourself, John Alden," said Demetrios. "That's not all I want to know. What's the story with Leslie, anyway?"

I protested. "I didn't say—"

"Hey, your face said it," Ippolito broke in. "The point is, you didn't have to keep it secret. If you want to hang out with Freeze instead of us, that's your business."

"I didn't say that either. And neither did my face."

"The proof of the pudding is in the pie, as Ms. Livingstone always says. You were with Leslie instead of with us. You're saying you really wanted to be at the meeting, but you couldn't possibly tear yourself away from her torrid embrace?"

"Look, Joe, we're supposed to be friends. What do I have to do, get down on my hands and knees and kiss your feet and swear on a stack of Chipiritos that I really think the Obnoxious Jerks are more important than Leslie Freeze?"

"Sounds like fun to me," Daley interjected. "Go ahead."

"Friends don't keep secrets," said Ippolito.

"Friends don't pull this kind of crap," I said. "I don't know what it is about Leslie that gets you so weird, but every time her name comes up, you go half nuts. I know I came in late. Am I missing something here?"

Now it was Ippolito's turn not to say anything.

"Hey, I don't want to interrupt a fine argument." Daley pointed to his watch. "But if we don't get over there to the theater, we'll all be missing something."

I sighed. "You and Wrist go get the tickets. We'll meet you over there in a couple of minutes."

"Personally I think this is more interesting than the movie," Demetrios said.

"Go," Ippolito ordered. "Back's right."

"You guys need our money?" I asked.

"Got you covered," said Daley, making a gun out of his thumb and forefinger. "Just pay us back when you get there. No rubber checks accepted. And hurry up. We don't want to miss the thrilling beginning."

Daley and Demetrios left. "All right. What's the story?" I asked Ippolito.

He tapped on the table and took a nibble out of his dead taco. "Not much of a story," he said finally. "Freeze

130

and I go back to elementary school. Second grade, I think."

"So?"

"So nothing. We used to play together till she moved away to the other end of town. That was in like sixth grade. So last year we hooked up again here at UGH. And she was mad at me."

"Why?"

"I don't know. All right, I do know. Some stunt I pulled in elementary school that really embarrassed her."

"What?"

"Something, I don't know. I don't even remember."

I could tell from the look on his face that wasn't exactly the truth. "You remember, all right."

"All right, I do remember. It was kind of gross. I don't really want to talk about it."

"Hey, come on. Don't get me all interested and then just clam up! What was all that stuff about friends not having secrets?"

"And what was all that stuff about some things not being anybody else's business? Look, Frank, what can I say? It's in the past. It embarrasses me, okay? I don't want to talk about it."

"Did you ever tell Leslie that? Apologize?"

"Yeah, sort of."

"Well, did you or didn't you?"

"I tried."

"Maybe you should try again."

"Look, now you know. I probably should've told you before."

"You're right. You probably should have."

"Does she still want to join?"

I nodded.

"Well, look, the point is, I'm one of the founding fathers of the Obnoxious Jerks. Aside from all those good reasons we already discussed why Leslie could be a problem as a member—and those are what's really important as far as I'm concerned—it would also be really awkward for me if she joined. Okay?"

"Not exactly. I still think she'd be a great member. I'm going to ask the other guys what they think."

"I can save you the trouble. The only people who would vote for her are you, Sims, Schwarzkopf, and maybe The Schneid."

I thought about it. "So she's one vote short, huh?"

"Right."

"What if I can convince somebody to abstain? Say, Demetrios."

Ippolito snorted. "Dream on!"

"What if?" I pressed.

"A tie has to be broken by the vice president."

"I get it. We don't have a vice president."

"I shouldn't tell you this, but actually we do."

"Who?"

Ippolito reached into his pocket and handed me a nickel.

I shook my head. "I don't get it."

"Vice President Thomas Jefferson. He was good enough to be the second vice president of this great nation, and he's good enough for the Obnoxious Jerks."

"I still don't get it."

"Vice presidents of the United States don't have any real duties except to vote in case of ties in the Senate. So we've given old Thomas the same job in the Obnoxious Jerks. Heads, he votes yes. Tails, it's no."

I smiled. "We must be the only club with a vice president and no president."

"Could be," Ippolito said. "So anyway, even if you manage to get somebody to abstain, you still have to get past old Thomas here. And I really wish you wouldn't try."

"I hear you," I said. "I just don't know what to do about it."

"Hey, we'd better get moving." Ippolito glanced at his watch. "We really don't want to miss the beginning. There's supposed to be a great opening scene."

The only great thing about the movie was the size of a couple of the women's breasts, which reminded me of my conversation with Leslie that afternoon. If she'd heard the hoots and whistles from the crowd when these chesty babes came on the screen, she'd have decided she was absolutely right about guys' attitudes.

Otherwise it was just another dumb spy movie with a few snappy lines and a whole bunch of car chases. None of us could figure out why we bothered to go to these things. After all, just driving home with Demetrios was a lot cheaper, almost as exciting, and twice as scary.

18

The rest of the weekend I was kind of worried about what I'd say when I ran into Leslie in La Feldstein's class. As it turned out, I didn't have to worry at all. Leslie and I kind of grinned at each other and said hello in a half-embarrassed way, but before we had a chance to say anything else, kids from the class started coming up and telling her how great she'd been at the talent show and what a rip-off it was that she hadn't won.

Actually, it was the guys who were harder to deal with. Alton got on my case first thing in homeroom, but I shut him up by asking where all his hot girlfriends were. By the time I hit the lunchroom, the Obnoxious Jerks were hot to find out every last detail about my afternoon with Leslie. Talk about obnoxious: Where did we go? What did we do? Did I go up to her room? Did I get another date?

For a while I held out and refused to answer, but I finally just gave up and answered yes to everything.

Yes, I was madly in love with her. Yes, she was pregnant. Yes, we were going to get married. Eventually the joke got boring and somebody changed the subject. But believe me, there is no such thing as privacy in high school.

A couple of days later things got hot. I'm talking about the weather. It was really hot. Also humid. The forecasters on the news were saying things like "record heat wave" and announcing something called the "discomfort index" and warning people to stay out of the sun to avoid heatstroke.

It didn't bother me at first, because I was kind of used to it. When I'd lived down South, heat and humidity were part of the territory pretty much all the time from early spring to late fall. But we had ways of dealing with that, ways like air-conditioning. And light clothes.

Unfortunately, when UGH was built, probably nobody had ever heard of air-conditioning. And as for clothes, there was no way you could violate the dress code. T-shirts were out. Shorts were prohibited. The idea seemed to be Coach Arborio's claim that sweating would build character.

After the first day of the heat the building was unbelievable. You passed by the gym, and you were nearly bowled over by the smell. Classrooms near the Dumpsters took on this horrible rotting-food stench. There were actually lines to use the sinks in the lavatories. A lot of people just couldn't wait and stuck their heads under the drinking fountains, so their drains backed up with ugly clumps of hair. In class we all used papers and magazines and anything else we could think of for fans. A couple of teachers brought electric fans from home, but they didn't help much.

"No end in sight," the newscasters insisted after the second day. "High pressure off the coast is pumping hot air up from the Gulf of Mexico, bringing no relief from the record heat and humidity for at least the next three days."

It got to be so bad we Obnoxious Jerks held a special powwow the day before our official Friday meeting. The issue was whose house had the best air-conditioning combined with the shortest walk from school. The last thing anybody wanted to do was walk clear across town in this heat. I offered to have the meeting at my house, but everybody remembered how my little sister Jenny kept breaking into the meeting the last time, so that was out. Ippolito said his parents absolutely refused to leave the air-conditioning on when nobody was home, so it always took his place two hours just to cool down. Daley finally agreed to have the meeting at his house, provided somebody else assumed responsibility for the Chipiritos.

At the meeting we went through half a dozen huge bottles of Doola Cola in about ten minutes. After his last mission to the fridge Sims announced we'd wiped out Daley's entire supply of ice. However, he'd noticed a couple of half-gallon cartons of ice cream in the freezer.

"No way," Daley said. "Just forget 'em. Those are for our dinner."

"Right," The Schneid snorted. "Two cartons of ice cream. Dinner for three."

"I'm serious," Daley said. "My parents are strict about that. What's in the freezer is off limits. You want ice cream, go to the supermarket. Or the Day/Nite."

"Go out there in the four o'clock sun without a car?" asked Ippolito. "The heat must be frying your brain."

"It's got to be thirty-five out there," said Perry Wu.

"Thirty-five?" Daley asked.

"Celsius," said Sims. "Be scienterrific."

"The humidity's scienterrific too," Schwarzkopf noted.

"Is there anybody around here who'll deliver ice cream?" The Schneid wondered. "You know, like a pizza?"

"Yeah, right," said Garcia. "Delivered in our patented warming ovens. By the time it gets here, you've got ice cream soup."

"Hey, the pizza's always cold by the time you get it," Ippolito pointed out. "So maybe . . ."

"I've got ice cream at my house," Demetrios said.

"Great. All the way the other side of town," Sims snorted.

Demetrios shrugged. "We could move the meeting over there."

"Forget it," Daley said. "You guys'll just have to do without."

"Can we get back to new business?" Schwarzkopf demanded.

"I guess," Daley said. "Even your new business is better than listening to these guys whine about ice cream."

"It's not just ice cream in that freezer," Sims announced. "It's heavenly hash."

"Why didn't you say so before?" asked The Schneid. "Hey, Planet, we'll chip in and buy it from you."

"Forget it," Daley said. "My parents hate shopping. I'm not going to get stuck to go all the way up to the supermarket or even the Day/Nite in this heat just so you guys can pig out."

"All for one, and one for all," Sims grumbled.

"New business," Schwarzkopf repeated. "I guarantee this will make everybody feel cooler."

"Recognized," said Perry Wu, who was today's chairman.

"I move we name Slush Puppies the Official Iced Glop, Shampoo, and Jockstrap Liner of the Obnoxious Jerks."

"Come on," Ippolito groused.

"Hey, sounds okay to me," said Daley.

"Schwarzkopf still has the floor," Perry Wu reminded us.

"Thank you," said Schwarzkopf. "This is a special temporary nomination, which takes effect only on those days when the temperature tops eighty-five degrees."

"Do I hear a second?" Wu asked.

"Wait a second," said The Schneid. "Do you hear that?"

"Very amusing," Ippolito remarked.

"Seriously," said The Schneid. "Shut up a minute."

We all did. Then we heard it. It was a weird tinkly sound that caused an instant reaction—the ice cream truck!

"I move a ten-minute recess!" said The Schneid.

"Wait! I've got the floor!" said Schwarzkopf.

"Seconded on the recess," said Ippolito.

"All in fa—" said Wu, but a chorus of "Aye"'s drowned out the rest of the sentence.

"Relief!" The Schneid shouted, and headed for the front door with the rest of us close behind. But as soon as he opened the door, he stopped running as though he had run into a brick wall. "After you, gents. No sense rushing into hell."

And it was hell out there. Man, it was hot! Brutal. When we flagged down the ice cream truck, the ice cream guy looked almost disappointed to see us, because it meant he had to step out of his air-conditioned truck and into the heat. We were lucky The Schneid had sharp hearing, because half the neighborhood swooped down on the truck a minute later.

As the line at the truck began to stretch halfway down the block, we trooped back into the house licking our Chocolotsas and Moonrock Bars and Big Pigs. Daley was waiting for us with a big roll of paper towels. He tore off a couple for each of us as we came in the door.

"Listen, you guys," he instructed, "use the towels. Or your pants, I don't care. If anybody drips on the carpet or the furniture, you're going to meet your doom."

"Also known as Madame Daley," said Joe Ippolito. "Doom personified."

"Can the meeting come to order again?" Wu inquired once we'd all settled down with drippy ice cream bars in our hands and paper towels on our laps.

"Go," said Sims.

"All right. Do I hear a second for Schwarzkopf's motion?"

"I don't know about Slush Puppies," said Daley. "Why not Slurpees?"

"I amend my motion," said Schwarzkopf. "I move we name Slush Puppies and Slurpees the Official Iced Glops, Shampoos, and Jockstrap Liners of the Obnoxious Jerks."

"Seconded," said Daley. "Humor the guy."

The motion passed unanimously. "More new business?" asked Wu.

"Anybody got any ideas for a new jerk-out?" The Schneid inquired.

"I know a good reason for one," said Robert Garcia. "The dress code's bad enough the rest of the year, but now it's ridiculous."

"I can live with a regular shirt," Ippolito agreed. "But long pants? It's crazy!"

"Hear, hear." Schwarzkopf waved his Cosmic Cone in agreement.

"I mean, come on," I said. "What are they afraid of?"

"Inflaming passion and lust," said The Schneid. "The next part is 'Skirts must cover thighs to the top of the knee.' "

"Right. They're afraid we might be subjected to El Gigundo's thighs in the flesh," said Ippolito. El Gigundo was this weird pinheaded kid who was so fat he had to go in sideways to make it through the classroom doors.

"So what's the jerk-out?" Daley asked.

"We could all wear winter coats," Demetrios suggested.

"Dying of asphyxiation does not strike me as an effective protest," said Schwarzkopf.

"We could wear shorts anyway," Sims suggested. "Under our pants. Get through the front door and strip the pants off."

"Right, and get sent to Crawley's office in about fifteen seconds," said Demetrios.

"You hardly even know what the inside of Crawley's office looks like," Daley reminded him.

"Hey, maybe it'd be like the shirt jerk-out: He'd make us wear our gym pants around—you know, shorts!" said Schwarzkopf.

"There's an idea," Wu said. "We could all walk around in our gym shorts."

"Too corny," Garcia decided. "And they'd shut that down in a hurry too."

"Hey," I said, totally joking. "Maybe we could wear skirts."

"As long as they cover our thighs," said Schwarzkopf, going along with the gag.

"Oh, yeah, sure," Demetrios muttered sarcastically.

"Get serious, Back," said Garcia.

"I can just see you walking around in a skirt," said Sims.

"Hey, quit beating up on him," Ippolito said. "It's only perfect, that's all."

Everybody stared at him. Including me.

"No kidding," he said. "Great idea, Back. Seriously."

Now that somebody was taking it seriously, I wasn't so sure. "You think so?"

"Great idea!" Ippolito repeated in a tone that was

half straight and half sarcastic. "Brilliant idea. It's perfect!"

"If you want to walk around in a skirt, it's perfect," said Demetrios.

"No. No kidding." Ippolito was getting all enthusiastic. "This is great. This is the perfect jerk-out. Hey, where in the official dress code does it say one word about guys wearing skirts?"

Everybody stared at him again.

"Nowhere, that's where. We can wear skirts and still be perfectly within our rights according to the dress code."

"As long as they're no higher than the top of the knee," Schwarzkopf reminded him.

"Right," said Ippolito. "It's fabulous."

Everybody stared at him some more. Then Schwarzkopf said, "I'm for it."

"You would be," Demetrios snorted.

"What's the story, guys?" Ippolito taunted. "Not man enough to wear a skirt for a couple of days? Here we've got the perfect setup, and you're chicken?"

"All right," said The Schneid. "I'm in too. But forget about panty hose."

"Hey, it's too hot for panty hose. Even the cheerleaders don't wear panty hose in this weather," Schwarzkopf pointed out.

"Or underpants, so I hear," said Ippolito. "But I won't go that far either. Come on, guys. Who else?"

"All right," said Garcia. "I give up. I'm in."

"That makes four of us. Come on, the rest of you guys," Ippolito urged.

"Well, I'm definitely opposed," said Demetrios. "You know what my father would do if he saw me prancing around in a skirt?"

"Something that would make the skirt almost appropriate, I'll bet," said Sims. "All right. Stay out if you want. I'm in."

"How about you, Perry?" Ippolito demanded.

Perry Wu had a resigned look on his face. "All right, all right. Fine."

"Planet?"

"I'm already trying to figure out where I'm going to get the damned thing," Daley said.

"And you're in, right, Back?"

I kind of made a face.

"Come on. It was your idea!"

"All right, all right," I said. "But I've got the same problem as Planet. How are we going to make this thing happen?"

"That's the next step," said Ippolito.

"Should we form a skirt committee?" Perry Wu asked.

"Forget it," Ippolito said. "There's no time. We've got to put this in motion right away. We've got to mobilize. This whole thing would look incredibly stupid the day after the heat breaks."

"So that means we've got to figure it all out now, so we can do it on Monday," I remarked.

"You got it," said Ippolito.

"Talk about rush jobs!" The Schneid said.

"As they say in the Navy, ship up or shape out," said Ippolito. "Now, who can we get to help us find the skirts?"

"Like your moms?" Demetrios taunted.

"My mom would probably go for it," said Sims. "I bet we're pretty close to the same size."

"Speak for yourself, pal," said The Schneid. "My mom would have fits if I asked her, and I'm like a foot taller than she is, not to mention a whole lot skinnier."

"My mom has the sense of humor for it," Schwarzkopf said thoughtfully. "And I'd guess she's about my size. The only problem is she lives in Alaska."

"How about sisters?" The Schneid urged.

Three of us groaned. "You don't have a sister, do you?" asked Daley.

"No," said The Schneid.

"Right," said Daley. "That's why you even bothered to suggest it."

"Yeah," I agreed. "Forget about it. Sisters, no way."

"We could just go buy the skirts," Garcia suggested.

"Oh, yeah, right," said Schwarzkopf. "We don't even know our sizes. What are we going to do, try them on? Probably get arrested for going into the dressing rooms."

"We might just have to try it," Ippolito said. "So far, we've got one skirt, maybe, for Wilver here."

"That's a pretty good jerk-out in itself," Schwarzkopf pointed out.

"Could be," Sims said, "but believe me, it won't happen unless the rest of you guys join the fun."

"So who knows anybody who can help us? Grandmothers? Aunts? Cousins? Friends?" Ippolito said.

Everybody shrugged or just sat there.

"Come on, gang. Somebody must know somebody."

Then I got an idea. "I do."

Ippolito shot me the nastiest, most pitiful look I have ever seen on the face of a friend.

19

"Leslie?" I said nervously. I was using the Daleys' kitchen phone. I had made the rest of the Obnoxious Jerks promise not to listen in at the door or pick up the extension in Planet's room. This was a delicate mission, and the last thing I needed was "help" from the guys.

"Frank?" Leslie asked.

"Yeah," I said.

"Delightful to hear from somebody who pretty much ignored me all week."

"Ignored you?" I didn't think I'd ignored her. We talked quite a bit all week. We still couldn't figure out the name of that damned dog.

"Yeah," she said. "If you're calling to ask me out this weekend, you really ought to learn some manners. Friday afternoon's a little late."

I felt about two inches tall. I hadn't even thought about asking her out. Not that it sounded like a bad idea; it just wasn't something I was used to thinking about. Harold Bergdahl would have called Leslie first thing Sunday night. Me, I wasn't that bright. Maybe it was just the heat. "It's not about a date," I said.

"I wasn't actually going to refuse or anything." Leslie sounded slightly deflated.

"Look, we can talk about that later. That's not really why I called. Actually I have some good news."

"Don't tell me. You're going to come over and fix our air conditioner."

"I don't think so."

"Then you don't have good news."

"Wait till you hear what it is."

"If it's not about the air conditioner, forget it. Ours just went out, and this place is broiling. The first thing I did when I got home was take off all my clothes and jump into the shower."

"Interesting."

"Filthy mind."

"Yeah," I said, and then I heard a click on the other end of the line. "All right, you guys, off the phone," I said.

"Wait a minute," Leslie said. "What's going on?"

"I'll explain in a second," I said to Leslie. "Come on, you guys," I said to whoever was on the other phone. "You promised."

"We promised not to use the phone in my room," Daley said. "We didn't promise anything about the one in my parents' room."

"Planet, either get off the line or forget the whole thing."

"I thought you might need moral support," Daley said.

"What is this, some kind of joke?" Leslie demanded.

"I'll explain everything in a second," I said. "Planet, off. Now."

"Okay, okay," Daley said. "But you'd better come through on this."

145

"Come through on what?" Leslie asked.

"One second," I said. "Planet!" I screamed. Then I heard the phone click off and the connection with Leslie get better. People with little sisters get to be experts at this stuff. "Sometimes . . ." I sighed.

"What is going on?" Leslie demanded.

"I'm at our meeting. You know, the Obnoxious Jerks?"

"If you're trying to rub it in, I'll just hang up now."

"Honest, I'm not. I think you've got the chance you wanted. You know, to join us?"

Leslie's voice brightened a little. "Really?"

"Here's the deal. We've got this really neat jerk-out planned, and we think maybe you can help."

"I thought you said the group had everything it needed without girls."

"I didn't say that. Other people may say that, but I didn't. I said I thought you should be a member."

"Yeah?"

"Yeah. I told you that. And now I think you've got your chance."

"How?"

I explained how tired we were of the dress code and how we wanted to protest the no-shorts rule. Then I told her about our idea of having the Obnoxious Jerks show up at school in skirts Monday morning.

Leslie laughed so hard I heard a funny thump and then dead silence at the other end of the line. She might actually have fallen out of her chair. "You okay?" I asked.

"Yeah, I'm fine. It's hysterical. I love it."

"It was my idea," I said, kind of wanting to impress her. "Sort of."

"Well, it's a great idea."

"Yeah, except we can't exactly go out to the mall

and go into The Limited, or wherever it is you girls hang out, and say we want to buy skirts."

"I'll say." Leslie laughed. "They'd probably call security and have you thrown out."

"And we couldn't afford it even if they didn't. So we need to find some skirts we can borrow for a day or two."

"And that's where I come in?"

"Right."

"I think my clothes would be a little small for you guys."

"Well, we figured you might be able to get them some other way. From your mom or your friends or somebody."

Leslie paused a second. "Maybe I could. But why should I?"

"Because I think it would probably get you into the Obnoxious Jerks."

"Probably? Probably? You've got to be kidding. I'm supposed to spend my entire weekend putting you guys in skirts so you can goof around in school Monday morning, and all you can say is it would *probably* get me into the Obnoxious Jerks. Probably isn't good enough, Frank."

"Well, I can't personally guarantee anything."

"I can. I can personally guarantee you I won't lift a finger for your friends unless I get a promise that I can join. And you can tell them I said so."

I sighed. I had already told the group that would be what she'd say. "Can I also tell them you'll be able to get the skirts?"

"You mean if I decide I want to?"

"Yeah."

"How many skirts are we talking about?"

"Seven or eight."

"Seven or eight! For that you should elect me president!"

"We don't have a president. Can you get that many skirts or not?"

"I'll have to make some phone calls."

"Yes or no."

"You have Allander. Nothing's either yes or no."

There's nothing like having your own words thrown back at you. "This is the first time in recorded history," I said.

"Okay, then. Yes. Somehow. If I can join."

"All right. Are you going to be around for a while?"

"I was going to go over to the library to get out of this heat."

"Just stay there. I'll go back to the meeting and see what they say. I'll call you back as soon as I can, so stay there till I do."

"Okay, but hurry up. It is sweltering in here. I'm going to find some shade and aim the garden hose at my body."

"Just don't go far from the phone."

"I won't."

"Okay. I'll talk to you soon."

I could hear the guys in the living room arguing and wisecracking about the best strategy to get the maximum publicity out of this jerk-out without getting ourselves beaten up or suspended or worse. Everybody looked at me as I walked in.

"Well?" Daley asked.

"Thanks a lump, Planet," I said. "It's nice to know I can depend on you when you make a promise."

"I told you, I never promised not to use the phone in my parents' room. A promise is a promise."

"Can she do it or not?" Perry Wu asked.

"She can do it, all right," said Schwarzkopf. "The question is who she'll do it with."

I glared at Schwarzkopf. The last thing I needed right now was a lame joke. "It's exactly what I told you.

She says she can probably get the skirts. But she won't unless we promise to make her a member."

"Well, we'll just get the skirts somewhere else, then," Ippolito said, giving me a very dirty look.

"I didn't hear you make any great suggestions," Sims noted.

"I'll think of some," Ippolito replied.

"Well, while you do, let's take a little poll," said The Schneid. "Who's in favor of letting her in?"

I raised my hand. Schwarzkopf raised his. Wu kind of half-raised his.

"Are you for or against, Perry?"

"Jeez, I don't know."

"Come on, Perry," The Schneid urged. "For or against?"

"I'm just thinking about how stupid I'll look in a skirt," Wu said.

"Pretty stupid, all right," Schwarzkopf noted. "But that's not the issue here."

"I don't know," said Wu. "Isn't it going to be kind of weird having a girl around for all our meetings?"

"Depends on the girl," said Schwarzkopf.

Perry shrugged. "Okay. I'm for her, I guess."

"What about you, Sims?" Schwarzkopf demanded.

"I'm against discrimination on general principles," Sims announced. "So I'm in favor. *If* she delivers the skirts."

"Does that mean I'm supposed to tell her she has to produce before she can join?" I asked, shuddering at the thought.

"Damn straight," said Sims. "She has to earn her way in."

"Yeah. Just like we did, right?" I said sarcastically.

"Who knows?" said Perry Wu. "She might trick us or something. She might say she can get the skirts when she actually can't. I agree. We make her an honorary member once she gets us the stuff."

"What's this 'honorary' business?" I demanded. "She's either a member or she isn't."

"Back's right, Perry," said The Schneid, taking a nickel from his pocket. "Even old Tom the J here is a full-fledged member with all rights, privileges, and duties of an Obnoxious Jerk. Sometimes he even helps pay for the Chipiritos."

"I don't know . . ." Wu replied.

"You want to take back your vote?" Ippolito asked eagerly.

Wu thought it over. "Yeah." He shook his head. "I guess she's probably okay. But I think we should make her an honorary member first."

"Aw, come on, Pair," Schwarzkopf urged. "Forget this 'honorary' crap."

"I think Wu's right," said Garcia. "Make her an honorary member, and if she turns out all right, she can join for real."

"Right," said Wu.

"I'd go for that deal," Daley announced.

"I'm not so sure Leslie would," I pointed out.

"Try it," said The Schneid. "If she gives us a flat-out no, we'll take another vote."

"I'm against it, period," said Demetrios.

"You're against the whole skirt idea too," Schwarzkopf reminded him.

"Can we vote on the honorary membership idea?" asked Wu. "Show of hands in favor?"

Everybody put a hand up except Demetrios and Ippolito. Schwarzkopf put up two. "I move we make it unanimous," he said.

"No way!" Ippolito insisted. The way he said it reminded me of the part of *Snow White* where Doc or Grumpy or one of the dwarfs starts complaining about "wimmen!" Then I remembered basically Grumpy or whoever it was was right: The first thing Snow White did was clean up the place and made the dwarfs wash their faces and do all sorts of neat little sweet domestic things that made them want to throw up. I was thinking how Leslie might end up being our Snow White, but then I remembered that whole story was pretty old stuff. Today, Snow White would probably go to work in the mine and leave the little guys home to run the dishwasher.

"You sound negative on this," said The Schneid.

"Then I made my feelings clear," Ippolito said.

"Does that mean you won't go along with the jerk-out?" The Schneid inquired.

"Two separate issues," said Ippolito. "The jerk-out I support one hundred percent. I just don't think it's worth changing the entire history of the Obnoxious Jerks over them. But you guys voted for it. I'll live with it."

"That's assuming Leslie is willing to take the deal," I pointed out. "She might just tell us all where to shove our 'honorary' membership. And our skirts."

But she didn't. Oh, she got a little huffy when I told her how she wouldn't become a member until she delivered the skirts, and then she'd only be an honorary member at that. But I kept telling her an honorary member was better than no member at all, and halfway to being a real member, and finally I wore her down. She demanded to hear the deal from at least one other member, so I had to drag The Schneid to the phone and have him explain the vote we had just taken, because Perry, our chairman of the week, was too shy to do it.

But after that she was all business. She'd already figured out a plan.

I reported to the assembled throng. We were supposed to come up with a place to meet that evening so she could take our measurements.

"Now there's an interesting development!" said The Schneid.

"I'd like to take *her* measurements," said Schwarzkopf.

"Thirty-thirty-thirty," said Daley. "What about her place?"

"Her air-conditioning's out," I said.

"Forget it!" most of us groaned.

"How about your place, Frank?" Garcia asked.

"Sure," I said sarcastically. "My sister would just love to watch."

"I think I can swing it," said The Schneid. "Make it seven-thirty. My parents have got some kind of dinner party to go to."

"Okay," I said. "Leslie also says we should bring five bucks each."

"Hey, wait a minute," Ippolito protested. "We asked her to help. We didn't say we'd hire her."

I gave him my most patient look. "She's going to need the money to buy the skirts."

"I thought she was going to get them from her mother or her friends or something," said Garcia.

"Get real," Schwarzkopf said. "We're all different sizes, and most of us are bigger than most of the girls in school. Nobody's mother's stuff is going to fit all of us."

"Exactly," I said. "So have your five bucks ready. IOUs and Monopoly money not accepted. And there's one last point. Leslie says we also need a place for sometime Sunday when we have to pick up the things and make last-minute alterations."

"Alterations? You mean you have to have alterations to wear a skirt?" Schwarzkopf grabbed his crotch and moaned.

"Very funny, Harry," I said tolerantly.

"Not me!" Schwarzkopf continued. "My cat had alterations, and look what happened to him!"

I ignored him. "Anybody want to volunteer a spot?"

"If all the skirts are going to be over at Leslie's place, seems to me that would make the most sense," said Wu.

"Their air-conditioning's broken, remember," Daley reminded him.

"Maybe they'll get it fixed by then," I said. "But I don't even know if Leslie would want to do it there anyhow. Somebody want to volunteer a backup?"

Schwarzkopf raised his hand. "Okay. Just don't mention a word of this to my cat."

I phoned Leslie with the news. And since no one was up for going out to play softball or anything else in the heat, that was pretty much the end of the meeting. Except that just before we adjourned, Ippolito got up and made this very serious speech about how this might be the last time we would all be together in this form, and he just wanted to say that if it didn't work out, the group had been really great while it lasted.

It was so touching that everybody shouted and threw Chipiritos at him. Everybody except Daley, who kept yelling, "Hey, guys, cut it out! My mom's going to kill me for this mess on the floor!"

20

All the way over to The Schneid's place that night, Ippolito kept hassling me about why of all the girls in school I had to pick Leslie to get interested in, and why I was so hot to impress her by ruining the Obnoxious Jerks, and why I had to bring up the idea of her helping us instead of figuring out a creative way of doing it ourselves, and what kind of friend was I anyway. I figured he'd eventually run out of gas, since he'd gone over pretty much the same ground on our way home, but apparently he had developed some kind of inner complaining-resource. So when we walked into The Schneid's living room a little after seven-thirty, I felt kind of relieved.

I looked around. Except for Demetrios and Garcia and Sims, the rest of the Obnoxious Jerks were already there, and then Garcia walked in from the bathroom. I figured Demetrios wasn't going to show up at all, and if Sims had managed to get a skirt from his Mom, he didn't really need to show up. That left only Leslie among the seriously missing. "Did she phone or anything?" I asked.

The Schneid shook his head.

"That figures," Ippolito muttered.

"You gave her the right directions?" The Schneid asked.

"Of course," I said. "Hey, it's only a little after seven-thirty. She'll be here."

Sims showed up a few minutes later. He claimed he took a closer look at his mom and decided there was no way one of her skirts would reach the top of his knees. That's what he claimed. The rest of us were positive he was too chicken to ask her.

"Where's Freeze?" he asked.

I looked at my watch. It was now 7:41. "Hey, Flash," said The Schneid, "maybe you should phone up to see if she actually remembered."

I went into the kitchen and dialed Leslie's number. Her phone rang about ten times, but nobody answered. I checked the number and tried again. Still nothing. Then I heard the doorbell ring. It had to be Leslie, so I headed for the living room.

But it wasn't Leslie. It was Demetrios. "You decided to join the fashion parade?" Ippolito inquired.

"Not me," Demetrios said. "I'm not courting death. I just thought I'd come by for a laugh."

"There must be something you can do this time, Wrist," said Sims.

"How about wearing a nice cool lemon meringue pie around your nose?" Demetrios offered. "Or I can get an assortment of pies, color-coordinated to match your outfits."

"You're a real pal," said Garcia.

"Hey, Back, did you get through to your little friend?" Ippolito demanded.

I shook my head. Ippolito tapped his finger on the face of his watch.

"Is that supposed to be some magic way of getting her here?" I inquired.

And then the doorbell rang and Demetrios answered it. Leslie stood there, drenched with sweat and slightly out of breath. She didn't say anything. All nine of us stared back at her. Then she gathered herself up and said, "Miss Freeze, were you waylaid by a band of Gypsies, or merely your own stupidity?" in a perfect imitation of Old Man Nilon.

The rest of us started cracking up as she turned back into a cowering student. "Sorry, sir," she squeaked in a childish voice. "Right," said Nilon-Leslie. "Stupidity. Take your seat."

She came in and flopped down on the arm of the sofa near the door. "Sorry I'm late, guys. It's the lamest excuse in history, but for some reason our tape measure wasn't in the sewing box where it always is. What can I say?"

"Say you'll have some Chipiritos," said Schwarzkopf, passing one of the bowls to her.

"Just had dinner. I pass."

"They're vegetarian," Sims pointed out.

"Thanks all the same," Leslie said.

"They're the Official Corn Chip of the Obnoxious Jerks," Schwarzkopf explained.

"Oh. Well. Maybe when I become an Official Member."

"Touché," said Wilver Sims.

"All right." She stood up and pulled a tape measure out of her pocket. "I need somebody to write stuff down. Who's got decent handwriting?"

"Back is just great," Garcia joked. "We actually thought of making him permanent secretary."

That's because we never take minutes. I am left-handed, and my penmanship has been described as

156

"chicken scratch," "cockroach trailings," and worse. "Very funny," I said.

"I'll do it," Daley volunteered.

Leslie handed him a notebook, opened it to a page with a little chart on it, and showed him where she wanted what. "Okay. Who wants to go first?"

"I'll go for it," Schwarzkopf said.

"Brave soul." She moved to the middle of the room. "Okay. Stand right here."

Leslie pointed right in front of her. Schwarzkopf stood there with a kind of embarrassed look while the rest of us hooted and made rude remarks.

"Okay," Leslie said. "Hands up."

Schwarzkopf put his hand on his wallet pocket. "Is this a stickup?"

"Come on," Leslie said. "I need to be able to measure your waist."

Schwarzkopf put his hands in the air, and Leslie fit the tape down toward Schwarzkopf's hips. "Careful, now,"

"Hey, hold still."

"I'm ticklish." Schwarzkopf giggled some more.

"Mama said there'd be days like this," Leslie said wearily. "Give me a break."

Demetrios and Garcia laughed and broke into a rendition of an old rock song called "Mama Said There'd Be Days Like This."

Leslie shouted a waist size at Daley, then moved the tape down toward Schwarzkopf's hips. "Careful, now," he said with a leer.

"Don't vorry, my tear," Leslie said in some weird accent. "Ve are going to make you bootifool."

After she finished with Schwarzkopf, Leslie had to put up with the rest of our wisecracks and waist sizes. Except when it was Ippolito's turn. Ippolito didn't say a word to her while she measured him, and "turn around" was about the extent of her end of the conversation. You could tell she regarded Ippolito about as highly as he regarded her.

I went last. Even though Leslie was all business, it felt kind of sexy the way she slowly put the tape measure around my waist and moved it down to my hips and then from my waist to my knee. But it's tough to feel all that sexy when people are standing around making wisecracks about you.

Leslie gave Daley the numbers, and when he wrote them down, the chart was full. Next she collected our money. Then she walked home with Sims and Demetrios, who lived over in her end of town. In a strange way I felt kind of jealous about that.

Ippolito must have picked up on it; he got in a little jab about watching out for those guys or they might just steal my girlfriend away. I just ignored him. Number one, she wasn't my girlfriend, and number two, those guys were the last ones likely to do any stealing. Yet the truth was I still felt jealous.

"She sure was a barrel of laughs tonight," Ippolito said sarcastically as we walked home.

"I thought it was pretty funny when she came in and did that Nilon imitation."

"Yeah. And then what? She didn't have anything to say except 'Stand here,' and 'Don't move.' "

"She said a couple of funny things."

"Too bad you can't remember what they were."

"I remember, and you do too. For one thing, she did those goofy accents and imitations."

"A laugh riot."

"Well, I don't remember you coming up with any classic zingers."

"Remember what I said? That we'd all end up quieting down when she was around? Well, that's just what we did."

"What planet were you on?" I said. "We were joking up a storm. The only person who didn't join in was you."

"Yeah, right. You guys were about as hilarious as she was."

I was all argued out. Whatever was eating Joe about Leslie was more than I could handle. I just let him rant on until I got home.

According to our plan, Leslie was going to work out the sizes of our skirts that night. I was supposed to meet her at her place at noon the next day so we could go buy them. My parents were busy, so I had to walk there. You can bet I was wearing shorts.

And was it ever hellish out there! Especially on her side of town, there wasn't any shade at all. It was so hot the soles of my shoes seemed to be melting. I was dead on my feet by the time I got to her house. I noticed the screen door was wide open, which meant the air-conditioning must still be out of whack. I rang the weird doorbell. This time it played "Jingle Bells."

"Be right there!" I heard through the screen. Leslie arrived at the door in a terry cloth bathrobe with her hair dripping wet. "Sorry. I got into that nice cold shower and I lost track of time. Come on in."

I did. She looked pretty good in that bathrobe. "Still no air-conditioning, huh?"

"They promised to come out and look at it this morning. Now it's afternoon."

"Do you have to wait around for them to show up?"

"No, my mom's out back. You want to meet her?"

I made a face. Meeting other people's parents is not one of life's biggest thrills. "What I really want is something cold to drink."

"There's tons of stuff in the fridge." She pointed toward the kitchen. "Help yourself. I'll be down in a second."

The refrigerator actually had a big bottle of Doola Cola, the Official Cola of the Obnoxious Jerks. We favored the underdog, and Doola Cola was about as much of an underdog as you can get. It was made in the area somewhere, so it was cheaper than Coke or Pepsi, and that was enough to win our official approval. The only problem was that it tasted lousy. I was surprised to see it in anybody's refrigerator but ours. I poured myself a glass. At least that familiar lousy taste was wet.

Eventually Leslie pulled herself together, and we took a horrible overheated bus downtown. Now that everybody goes to the air-conditioned malls, about all that's left of downtown Froston is a couple of sad-looking hardware stores, a really lame old department store, and half a dozen bars. It's pretty seedy. But it's also got a few thrift shops where they sell old used clothes. Leslie figured they'd be the cheapest places to buy all the skirts we needed.

Leslie had hung around the thrift shops a lot. She said she sometimes browsed through them when she wanted special costumes for her drama class. She knew that the right sizes weren't always printed on the tags, and she brought her notebook and tape measure along so we could make sure of what we were buying. We didn't even walk into the first two thrift shops we passed, because Leslie knew they'd be useless. But when we went into the third place, we made our way around all sorts of superstrange suits with enormous lapels and weird lacy dresses that looked as if they came straight out of some ancient Western movie. Eventually we found the racks of skirts.

"Lucky we're not fussy," Leslie said when she saw the selection we had to choose from.

"What do you mean?" I joked. "We're not going to school in anything less than a Lordette would wear."

"Then I should have collected a hundred bucks from each of you, and we could have gone out to the Classic Galleria."

The Classic Galleria was the fancy expensive mall in the really exclusive suburb where all the snobby kids shopped. "All right," I said. "I guess we'll settle."

Leslie had a really skeptical eye as she looked through the piles of skirts. "Check this out." She held up this awful thing that had an alternating pattern of little hearts and "Hot Stuff!" in tiny letters. I made a face.

"Perfect." She tossed it over her arm. "Just Ippolito's size."

"You bring that back, and you are not likely to survive the weekend. What's with you two, anyway?"

She shrugged and ignored my question so completely she might not have even heard it. "How about for you? Might have to move the buttons a little."

"That would be a cold day in hell."

We looked some more. It was really amazing what people actually wore. Or maybe they didn't really wear this stuff; maybe somebody had given it to them as presents, and they realized it was so awful they couldn't think of anything else to do but to give it away, pronto. There were skirts in combinations of bright orange and deep purple and puke green, stuff you couldn't imagine anybody in her right mind wearing. Yet there they were on the rack or in the pile. And usually something even worse was right beside them.

"Here are some that look about your size. Check this out." Leslie held up a bright red thing with a bright green palm tree painted on it. It was the kind of thing you'd wear if you wanted to attract guys. That was exactly what I didn't want to do.

I frowned. "That one's definitely not my size."

Leslie tossed it on top and started flipping through the pile again. "Hey, stop!" I said, spotting a nice quiet gray item. "How about that one?"

"I never took you for the preppy look."

"At least it doesn't look like it's trying to pick up guys."

"Forget it. It's wool. Not only will you swelter, you'll also scratch yourself to death." She went back through the pile, rejecting one skirt after the other. She finally found something in a very plain dull blue. "Here. This is you."

She held it up in front of me. "Sold?"

"Wait a minute. There's a big round stain on the side."

"Hey, this is a thrift shop, not a fashion emporium. You can live with the stain for a day or two."

I made a face. "Reminds me of that dog in the Little Rascals. You know, the ring around his eye."

Leslie grinned. "What *was* his name anyway?"

"Huey," I muttered. "Tommy."

Leslie shook her head. "Blackie? We've got to come up with it."

"Bunky. Sammy. Somethingy."

Leslie kept shaking her head. "Close. No dice. Anyway, what about the skirt?"

I looked at the stain again and shook my head.

"It's back to this, then." She whipped out the red palm-tree job.

"That stain is looking better and better."

The thrift shop was as hot as the rest of town. One way they kept their prices down was by skimping on air-conditioning. By the time we walked to the front of the store with eight skirts and one scarf—Leslie had found some funky thing out of the forties for herself—we both were wiped out. But Leslie still had enough energy to do a great job of bargaining. By pointing out some of the stains and stuff, she got the clerk to cut the prices on three or four of the items. In the end we actually managed to get all the stuff for less than the forty dollars we'd collected.

Then Leslie insisted on stopping off at this used-book store down the street, which was even hotter and mustier inside than the thrift shop. The tired old guy who ran the place recognized her the second we walked in. He handed her this used book by somebody I'd never heard of named Fred Allen. Even though the book looked really beat-up, it cost five dollars, but she forked over the money without trying to make a deal.

"Who is this Fred Allen guy?" I asked as we went out the door.

"A big comedy star on radio."

"Radio?"

"Yeah. Before TV. Most of the great TV comedians our parents knew came from radio. And some of them came from vaudeville. Or burlesque."

"I thought burlesque was where women took their clothes off."

"That too. But the comedy was almost as important as the strippers."

"Live and learn. So was this Fred Allen guy really funny?"

"Hilarious. Johnny Carson is a real fan of his. He has the Mighty Carson Art Players? Well, that's a direct rip-off of the Mighty *Allen* Art Players, which they did on radio. And in some ways David Letterman's show is kind of like what Allen was doing—regular characters, stuff like that."

"Man! You're really serious about this stuff!"

"Comedy is serious business," Leslie said with a kind of funny wiggle of her eyebrows and a flip of her imaginary Groucho Marx cigar.

We went into a little lunch counter down the street— air-conditioning at last!—and lingered over root beers until we got nice and cool. Leslie flipped through her book and read me some pretty funny comedy routines. She seemed real relaxed, but there was still one thing bothering me. "What's with you and Joe?"

"I don't want to talk about it," she said, very bristly.

"Seriously. Why don't you guys get along?" I pressed.

"Drop the subject," she said, staring hard into her

soda. Then she looked up at me again. "You really want to know?"

"Yeah. I really do."

Leslie stared at me even harder. "Let's just say your good friend pulled a dirty trick on me. I mean a really rotten one."

"How bad could it have been?"

"Real bad."

"What did he do?"

"He just humiliated me in front of my entire sixth-grade class. That's all I'm going to say about it. I really don't want to go into it."

"Didn't he apologize?"

"Apologize? Ippolito? Ha!"

"I can't believe he'd let something like this go on so long."

"Believe it. I mean, he sort of tried to make up once or twice, but he never actually said he was sorry. And as far as I'm concerned, he doesn't need to just apologize. He needs to grovel."

"Oh, come on."

"That's how I feel about it. And I mean what I said. Drop the subject."

I did. But that didn't mean I didn't want to know more about it.

21

It was still about a million degrees out as Ippolito and I walked over to Schwarzkopf's place Sunday night. "I've been talking to Leslie," I told him.

"Hot news bulletin!" Ippolito said sarcastically.

"She says you really humiliated her back in grade school."

"Did she tell you how? Or why?"

"No. Why don't you?"

"Because I don't feel like it. And I bet she forgot to mention the number she did on me first. I was just getting a little revenge."

"This sounds like second grade. You know, 'You hit me first!' 'No, you hit me first!' 'No, you did.' I don't care what happened. It's over. It's long gone. Why don't you two just make up?"

"We basically hate each other's guts, that's why. Personally I think the whole reason she wants to join the Obnoxious Jerks is to get back at me."

"What? Are you paranoid or something?"

"Just my own personal opinion."

I shook my head. "I don't know why I bother. You two are just too much. I give up."

"Good. Leslie and I are none of your business anyway."

"Maybe not. But somehow I have this crazy idea that it would be nice if two people I happen to like would quit carrying old grudges around."

"A noble sentiment, to be sure. Think on, my friend," Ippolito said as we arrived at Schwarzkopf's door and went inside. He glanced at Leslie and back at me. "Subject closed," he muttered.

A couple of minutes later Demetrios showed up. "What are you doing here?" Schwarzkopf asked him.

"What do you mean, what am I doing here?"

"You're supposed to be busy doing the picket signs. We don't have a skirt for you."

"That's just the way I want it," Demetrios said. "The signs are drying over at my place. I came over to lend moral support."

"Some moral support!" Schwarzkopf snorted. "You just came over to get a sneak preview of us in our skirts."

Demetrios just grinned.

Leslie handed Sims his skirt from the top of the pile. He held it out in front of him and scowled. "Green is definitely not my color."

"Small is definitely not your size," Leslie said. "We didn't have a whole lot of choice."

"Yeah," I pointed out. "It was either that one or a print that said 'Big Trouble' all over it."

Sims looked thoughtful. " 'Big trouble.' I like that. You should've gone for it."

"Believe me, Wilver, you didn't see the thing," Leslie said. "Bright orange letters on dancing elephants?"

Sims winced and nodded. "Maybe not."

Leslie passed out the rest of the skirts. We held them up to our waists and compared notes and made snide remarks such as "How cute!" and "Adorable!" and "Is this a product of the School for the Blind?" Then Leslie said, "Okay. Who goes first?"

Everybody just stood there. "Come on, guys," Leslie said.

Everybody still stood there. "Schwarzkopf. Go first," said The Schneid.

"Hey, I went first for the measuring," Schwarzkopf said. "Besides, it's my house."

"Let's move, guys," Leslie said. "Somebody has to go first."

Everybody stood there some more.

"How do you expect to wear these skirts to school if you haven't got the courage to wear them in front of your friends?" Leslie asked.

"Good question," Perry Wu muttered.

"Oh, I'll do it," I said finally. "We can't wait around here all night."

"My hero," Ippolito remarked with a ton of sarcasm.

"Where's the bathroom?" I asked.

"Men's or women's?" Schwarzkopf replied.

"So funny I forgot to chuckle," I said. "Where?"

Schwarzkopf pointed the way. I went in to change.

I took off my shoes and my pants and looked at the skirt. Then I realized something. "Hey!" I shouted through the door. "How do you put this thing on?"

"Quit stalling in there!" The Schneid shouted back.

"Seriously! Do you step into it or pull it over your head?"

"Step into it!" Leslie shouted back.

I did. It got up to my butt, but it wouldn't pull any farther. "You sure?" I shouted.

"Yeah!" Leslie shouted back.

This was getting to be incredibly frustrating. "It won't go on all the way!"

"Did you unbutton it first?" Leslie shouted.

Well, thanks. How was I supposed to know about that? I didn't shout anything back.

"Hey, Wess," Schwarzkopf hollered through the door, "you mean to tell us you didn't know you had to unbutton it? Jeez, what a dolt!" Everybody outside laughed.

I half laughed too. We weren't exactly up on these important technical points. I took the thing off, unbuttoned it, and stepped back in. This time it worked fine. I fastened the buttons again.

"Hey, let's get moving!" The Schneid shouted. "Did you strangle yourself with that thing or what?"

"Calm your buns!" I shouted back. I looked at myself in the mirror on the medicine chest over the sink. I had to stand up on tiptoe and lean way close to the mirror to see anything at all below my waist, but what I could see I sure didn't like.

I took a deep breath, turned the doorknob, and eased the door open—to a chorus of hoots and wolf whistles and blown kisses and remarks like "Hey, gorgeous!" and "Over here, sweetie!"

It was exactly what I expected, but that didn't prevent me from turning bright red. Then I noticed even Leslie was laughing at me.

"Would you mind telling me what's so funny?" I said with as much dignity as I could manage.

"I don't know what these guys think is so hilarious," Leslie said. "But I think it's pretty funny to see you wearing that skirt backwards."

Everybody had a good howl about that, and I took a lot more kidding. After that, things went pretty smoothly —if you can consider a houseful of kids making wisecracks smooth going. There was a lot of snickering and wisecracking and comparing how the skirts looked and felt and how weird it was to walk around in them.

But Leslie had been pretty accurate with her measurements, and we weren't exactly going for a fit so perfect it would knock everybody's eyes out, so she only had to do a couple of minor alterations where the buttons didn't quite close. Fortunately Ippolito's skirt fit just fine. That spared us having to watch Joe and Leslie square off again.

Once we'd all changed back into our shorts, Leslie refunded fifty-six cents to each and every one of us— except Demetrios, of course. We needed a place to meet in the morning, but Daley refused to volunteer his place again even though it was closest to school. He said it was going to be bad enough explaining to his brother and sister and parents why he was wearing this stupid skirt, and he absolutely wasn't going to explain why he was hanging out with a bunch of other idiots who were doing the same thing.

So we ended up agreeing to meet at Wu's place. Perry's parents had a long commute, so they left really early in the morning. That was just fine with us.

We'd covered everything, at least down to the top of our knees. All that was left was to go home and get some sleep. And hope we had enough courage to put our skirts on in the morning.

22

So that's pretty much the whole story of how I, a normal red-blooded American boy—okay, almost normal—found myself standing in front of the mirror staring at myself in a skirt the next morning. A while back I mentioned just how stupid it looked on me and how I decided to change my shoes to see what that would do. Well, when I finished changing my shoes, I took another look in the mirror. I looked like a stupid guy in a stupid skirt who had just changed his shoes.

I took two steps toward the door and almost fell on my face. Walking in a skirt is not exactly something that comes naturally. I mean, girls get years of practice.

I hesitated when I got to my bedroom door. This was not going to be easy. But I had to show myself sometime. I opened the door, and stepped out into the hallway. My sister Jenny stopped in her tracks and let out the kind of shriek you only hear in the most disgusting severed-heads-and-spilling-intestines horror movies. "Gross!" she screamed. "Unbelievably gross!"

"Shut up," I replied politely.

"I can't believe it! Mom! Dad! Quick! Frank's gone insane! Totally!"

I walked back into my bedroom in a dignified manner. Or as dignified as you can be when you're a guy wearing a skirt that doesn't quite fit and you're afraid you're going to trip over your own two feet.

"He's turned into some kind of pervert!" my sister shouted as I slammed the door. "You've got to come here and see!"

I gathered up my books and my homework and sat down at my desk with a sigh. "I'm telling you, he's got a skirt on!" Jenny shrieked in the hallway. "You've got to do something!"

"Fine," I heard my dad say through the door. "But I don't believe it's any of your business."

"It is if he walks around like that and embarrasses me in front of my friends," Jenny said. "I'd only die, that's all."

"You stay out of this," my father told her. He knocked on my door.

"Who is it?" I inquired.

"Dad. You mind letting me in for a second?"

Of course I minded. I minded plenty. But the truth was going to have to come out sooner or later. I stood up, tugged my skirt down, and walked over to unlock the door.

"Look! He's hiding!" my sister shouted.

This was true. It was bad enough having to deal with my parents without having to deal with Jenny at the same time. So I stayed right behind the door, out of sight, as I opened it. Once Dad came in, I closed it again.

My father took one look at me and made a face. "What do you think you're doing?"

I shrugged. "Getting ready for school."

"You know what I'm talking about."

I pointed to the skirt. My father winced and nodded.

"It's not what you think," I said.

"I'm not thinking what you think I'm thinking," he said.

"Well, that's good," I said. "Because it's not that at all."

"That's nice." He looked me up and down. "You want to explain, or do I have to guess?"

"I have to wear this to school, okay?"

"Okay. Fine. Groovy. What I want to know is *why*. Did you lose a bet? Are you in a play? What?"

Jenny opened the door and peeked in. "Get out of here!" I snapped.

"See?" she whined. "Told you!"

Dad turned toward her. "Out!" he snapped. "Now!" Jenny pointed her finger at me, giggled, and shut the door.

Dad turned back to me. "Where were we?"

"I can't tell you. I'm sworn to secrecy."

He stared at me again. "Well, all I can say is, wearing that outfit to school takes either a lot of stupidity or a lot of guts."

"Or a little of both," I said. "Honest, if I could tell you, I think you'd almost approve."

"But you can't."

"Not till tonight."

My father stroked his mustache. "All right. Just promise me one thing."

"What?"

"Try not to get the living crap kicked out of you, okay? Doctors are expensive."

172

When I got out to the kitchen, my mom was waiting to hound me. She didn't know why I was doing this, but she knew there couldn't possibly be any good reason. She just hoped that maybe someday I would grow up and learn that you can't just do as you please. I didn't even bother to argue. I had to save my energy for the rest of the day.

The phone rang. My mom picked it up—"It's Joe. For you." I went down the hall to take it in my parents' room.

Jenny walked in right behind me, giggling uncontrollably. "Yeah, yeah, I know," I told her. "It's a laugh riot."

"It sure is." She laughed and pointed at me.

"I've got a phone call. Get out of here."

She stood there, stared at me, and shook her head. I threw a pencil at her. "You're crazy!" she said. "You're nuts!"

I glared at her. She giggled some more, then left. "And close the door behind you," I snapped.

She did. I picked up the phone. "Okay, Mom, you can hang up." I waited till I heard the click.

"Just checking, Back," Ippolito said. "To make sure it isn't just me. Is this the stupidest thing you have ever done in your life, or what?"

"Hey, it wasn't my idea," I told him.

"The hell it wasn't."

"Sue me," I said.

"Do you look stupid, or what?" he asked.

"Three guesses."

"You'd better not back out now," he warned.

"Nobody'd better back out now."

"See you in ten?"

"Make it fifteen," I said. "I think I'm going to change this—"

173

"Oh, no, you don't."

"—pair of socks," I concluded. "Is that okay with you?"

"Wouldn't want you to look out of style or anything. Fifteen it is."

Fifteen minutes later I was sitting in my room, looking out my window, waiting for Ippolito to turn up. The sun was streaming in the window. It was going to be another broiling day, which for once was exactly what we wanted. And where was Ippolito? I went into my parents' room and phoned him.

But of course there was nobody home. He had to be on his way. On a normal day I might have gone out and walked up the street to meet him. Somehow today I just didn't want to.

I went back into my room and looked out the window again. A good-looking girl I sort of half recognized was on her way to school early for some reason. She was wearing a skirt that barely covered her knees. I was wearing a skirt that barely covered my knees. Somehow she looked a whole lot better. I took another look. It wasn't just her socks.

The phone rang. I kind of smoothed out my skirt, got up, and walked carefully across to my parents' room to answer it. I was beginning to get the hang of this.

"Hey, where are you?" Leslie's voice demanded. "Where's everybody else?"

"Who's there now?"

"Sims and Wu and me. That's it. Did you chicken out?"

"Hey, I'm sitting here in a skirt, okay? Does that sound like chickening out?"

"It does if all you do is sit there. Get over here."

"I'm waiting for Ippolito."

"Well, where is he?"

"He said he was on his way."

"Did you phone him to make sure?"

"Yeah, I phoned. There was no answer at his place. So he must have left already."

"Well, hurry up," she said urgently. "It's getting late."

"Look, I'll be over there in a few minutes. Even if I can't find Ippolito."

"You'd better."

"I just told you I'd be there. I'll be there."

"How do you look?" she said with a giggle in her voice.

"Like a bad comedy act."

I went to the front door, leaned out, and looked up the street. It was definitely another terrible day out there— totally unbearable. The heat and humidity hadn't let up one bit. So why was somebody off in the distance coming down the street with a long winter coat on?

Because a certain friend of mine didn't have as much guts as he thought he did, that's why. The mysterious person sweltering in the coat was exactly who I guessed it was: Joe Ippolito.

"Don't you look stunning!" he said as he came through the front door, kind of looking me up and down and pretending to take a peek up my legs.

"Seriously," I said.

"Seriously! Lots of girls in the class are going to die of envy."

"Very funny. I'd've said the same to you, except you chickened out and wore this coat. Some guts! I just hope you've got what you're supposed to have under there."

"I certainly do," Ippolito said with a leer.

"You know what I mean."

"You forget, my man. I'm the one at the end of the

175

line. I'm the one who has to start out first. No way am I going out there in a skirt all alone."

"Come on. Quit stalling. Let's see."

Ippolito coyly opened the coat, flashed me a look, and closed it again. "Come on," I repeated.

Joe took off the coat. He was wearing a striped tennis shirt with his green-striped skirt. They halfway matched, but the other half clashed so terribly it made you want to hide your eyes. "You don't look all that bad yourself," I lied.

"Not terminally stupid?"

"Not terminally," I replied. "But close."

"Is it me, or is it hard to walk in these things?"

"Are you kidding? When we get to school, I'm likely to take the entire staircase headfirst."

"We're just lucky high heels aren't part of the bargain," Ippolito said.

"Or panty hose."

"Just remember, this was your idea."

"I'm really going to forget when everybody on the planet keeps reminding me," I said sarcastically. "You going to wear that coat all the way to school?"

"Are you crazy? That was just for the first leg of the trip. For soloing. You ready?"

"Yeah, as soon as I call Leslie and let her know we're on our way."

"Is everybody over there already?" Ippolito asked.

I made a face. "Try 'nobody.' "

"Nobody?" he said in amazement.

"Well, Wu and Sims. And Leslie."

"Oh, great. I can just see it. Harry's dad saw the skirt and grounded him, and The Schneid's mom said, 'No way,' and Roberto's—"

"Let's not get paranoid. We're not exactly on time either. How about taking that coat to my room and tossing it on the bed so my mom doesn't freak out?"

"You want me to walk a whole extra hallway in this thing? I'll just hang it here in the closet."

"Fine." I went to the kitchen to dial Leslie's number.

"Hello?" she said.

"Joe's here. We're leaving right now."

"About time," Leslie replied. "Everybody's here."

"Already?"

"Everybody but you guys," Leslie said. "Hurry it up. It looks like the perverts' convention over here."

I went back out to the living room. "You go first," I said.

"Me? Why me?"

"I've got to lock up."

Ippolito gave me this horrible look. Then he shook his head, gathered himself together, and stepped bravely onto the porch. "Come on. The coast is clear."

"I'm just checking to make sure I've got my keys."

"Stalling," he said. "You're just stalling. Hurry it up! I see some kids way up the street."

"I'm not stalling. There aren't any pockets in this skirt. Where'd you put *your* keys?"

"In my purse, stupid," he joked, then stopped short. "Oh, man!"

I knew what he was thinking before he even said it. "Forgot 'em, right?"

Ippolito looked sheepish. "Oh, well. We keep a spare outside."

"What about your wallet?"

"That I've got!" he said confidently. Suddenly he looked slightly sick. "I think." He took his bookpack off his shoulders and looked in the outer pocket. Then he looked in the book compartment. "My dear," he said, "I'm sure you won't mind lending me the wherewithal for lunch."

"Delighted. Now, after you."

"No, my dear. I insist. After you."

We probably would've stood there all day, except those kids up the street really were getting close. So we gathered up our courage and hit the sidewalk. This was either going to be the biggest and best jerk-out of all time, or the absolute, total, and complete worst. Assuming we lived through it.

23

I was worried. Ippolito was worried. Everybody at Leslie's was probably worried. The weird thing was that we had no idea what we were worried about.

It couldn't be the insults. By now we were pretty sure we had heard every lame wisecrack about our knees and our thighs and our masculinity—we'd made them all ourselves. And we knew we were going to be in for trouble with the school administration, but we'd been through that before. So why did I feel as though I was going to be embarrassed and humiliated any second?

Well, for one thing, I still wasn't sure how to walk in a skirt without making a total fool of myself. We should have had Leslie give us lessons. "How did you act on the way over here?" I asked Ippolito.

"I acted like I had pants on under my coat."

That wasn't much help. "Any ideas about what to do now?"

"Cool is the word. Dignity at all times."

"Some dignity."

"Pretend you're Scottish." He broke into an accent. "You're wearing a manly kilt."

"What was that accent?" I teased. "The Italian part of Slobbovia?"

"You'd better just hope you don't have your manly kilt on backwards," Ippolito needled back.

"I just hope it doesn't fall down. You notice? There's no belt or anything to keep it up."

"Yeah, I noticed. Weird, all right."

"Hey, sweetie!" some guy yelled from a passing car. We turned to look. This enormous brain-dead dude with a tiny head and stubble for hair stuck his face out the window, puckered up his lips, and blew us kisses.

It wasn't exactly a surprise. We knew it had been just a matter of time till this kind of stuff started. All last night I'd wondered about how I'd react when it did. I was pretty positive I would turn bright red and slink away. But now I was just irritated. "There's the first idiot," I groaned.

Now the pinhead's friend was leaning out the window too. Both of them were blowing kisses at us. "I really feel like flipping him the finger," Ippolito said.

"Forget it," I told him. "We can't run fast enough in these damned things."

Lucky for us, it was still pretty early, and the going-to-school traffic was only just beginning. Even so, we felt like alien beings as we walked through the neighborhood. Younger kids kind of steered clear of us, mumbling comments we couldn't quite hear but didn't have much trouble guessing. A couple of little kids on their way to school were totally baffled. We could see them whispering to each other. Finally they came right up to us and said, "Are you boys or girls?"

Ippolito gave them a big insincere smile. "We're not allowed to tell."

Worse were the wise guys and even a couple of brain-dead girls who tried to taunt us with all the snide remarks we'd already come up with ourselves. The very worst were a couple of junior high boys who just wouldn't quit. They stared up our legs and yanked at our skirts, and finally the only thing we could do was lose our cool and start chasing them. We knew we couldn't catch them, and we didn't really try, but at least we got them off our case.

Somehow we managed to get to Wu's place without falling on our faces or getting beaten up or dying of embarrassment. When we went through the door, it felt as though we'd landed in a safety zone. But the living room looked like the perverts' convention, all right.

It wasn't just the skirts. It was also the fact that none of us had any real fashion sense. I mean, the skirts were bad enough. Combined with our knobby knees and ugly legs and the weird assortment of odd-colored shirts and socks and running shoes we wore, they really made us look like the nerdiest semihumans from the planet Nerd. Leslie and Demetrios were the only ones in the room who looked halfway sane.

"We've made a rule," Wu said. "No wisecracks. Everybody's already heard enough."

"Everybody but you, Wu," Schwarzkopf reminded him. "You've been in here the whole time. You haven't been out there in the real world yet."

"At least everybody's here," Leslie said, turning to me and Ippolito. "Your skirts okay?"

"How would we even know?" I asked.

"Just so they're not falling down or riding up or anything."

Ippolito and I just shrugged.

"They've got the look I don't want to know better," said Schwarzkopf, quoting from some old commercial.

"Okay, guys," said The Schneid. "We'd better get moving."

"Right. Everybody grab one of these things." Demetrios passed out the picket signs. He'd done a nice job on them. They were lettered very neatly in bright colors and said things such as **We Hate to Do This, but We Had to Leave Our Shorts at Home; We Can't Skirt the Issue—Let Us Wear Our Shorts; We're Cool—So Are Shorts;** and **Now You Know Why They Call It a 'Dress' Code.** As usual, Demetrios was the silent partner. He had no intention of walking in the picket line with us once we got to school.

"In unity there is strength," Planet Daley hollered as we summoned up our courage one more time and walked out the door. He was right. Even though we really looked more like obnoxious jerks, small *o*, small *j*, than ever before, there really was something strong and powerful about us as we marched to school wearing our skirts and waving our signs. When we'd been walking alone, everybody gave us dirty looks. Now we got more, plus some extra added evil remarks from assorted Lords and Viscounts and their henchpersons. But now that we had our little phalanx, we felt protected.

"It's great being able to shoot insults back at those cretins," said Planet Daley, thumbing his nose at one loudmouthed kid driving past.

"Just as long as we don't run into a gang of tattooed Lords on motorcycles," Leslie pointed out.

We expected hostility. What we didn't expect was that a lot of people—even some of the brain-dead seniors—actually were laughing *with* us, not at us. They started coming up and throwing their fists in the air and saying "Right on!" and "Go for it!" without any trace of a smirk, really meaning it. By the time we got to school, we'd already attracted a small crowd of supporters.

Now, we knew the rules. There was no protesting

allowed on school property. It said so right in the *Ullman Griswold Memorial High School Student Handbook* a couple of pages past the dress code. It wasn't a rule that anybody generally needed to pay much attention to, since the only time I could remember any protesting was when our brain-dead star running back got kicked off the football team for nearly flunking out, but we were positive the administration would take great pleasure in enforcing it.

So we kept our picket line across the street from the school entrance. That worked just fine. Between the way we were dressed and our picket signs and our shouts of "We want shorts! We want shorts!" we didn't have too much trouble attracting attention.

It was great. We just ignored the snottier remarks from the crowd that started gathering. But even some of the suck-up Student Council types who normally went down the line with the school on everything started arguing with each other about whether we were right. Good-looking girls who normally looked at us as though we were pond scum actually came up and said that they were on our side.

"Gutless creeps!" shouted one muscle-bound geek.

A girl I recognized from the cheerleading squad turned around and told him, "Gutless? Bet you don't have the guts to wear a skirt in public!"

The geek just grunted and walked away. "Go for it! Go for it!" the cheerleader and her friends yelled, almost as if it were fourth and goal.

Leslie was our lookout. Suddenly she wriggled her way through the crowd. "Get ready!" she hollered to us over our chants. "Here comes Arborio."

I looked. With that cocky strutting walk of his, Coach Arborio crossed the street and pushed the crowd aside. I could feel my heart start thumping.

"All right," Arborio said, standing in the middle of

our little parade. "Would somebody mind telling me what this is about?"

"I thought you had a college education," Schwarzkopf replied.

The crowd let out a loud laugh and a couple of whoops. "Comedy is always aggressive," Leslie whispered in my ear.

"What's the deal?" Arborio pressed.

"Read the sign, turkey!" somebody yelled—I think it was Ippolito—in the sort of squeaky-squawky voice the lame ventriloquist used at the talent show.

Arborio just stood there. "Okay, 'gents.' Who's the spokes'man' for this group?" He said "gents" and "man" in a snide tone that would start a fight under the right circumstances.

"The spokeskirt," said The Schneid to another volley of laughter and whoops of support.

"We all are," Sims replied.

Arborio folded his arms across his chest. "Well, skirts, how do you expect to get into school today?"

"Walk through the front door," said Garcia.

"Not in violation of the dress code, you're not," said Arborio.

"You're right for once," Ippolito responded. "We're not in violation of the dress code. We're not."

A couple of "Ooh"'s and hoots came from the crowd.

"Let me hear that again," Arborio said. "I'd like to know how you could possibly not be in violation."

"All our skirts come right to the top of our knees," Sims said. Following his lead, we extended our legs toward Arborio to prove it.

"Very funny," sniffed the Coach.

"Not at all," said Schwarzkopf. "It'd be nice to wear them shorter on a hot summer day like this, but the dress code forbids it."

"I hope you guys are planning to change before you

try to get into school. That's all I've got to say," Arborio said.

"Don't bet on it," replied Perry Wu. "That's all we've got to say."

Arborio stormed off without saying a word.

"Bunch of clowns!" one of the brain-dead shouted at us. I looked toward the voice. It was George Alton.

"Must be right," Schwarzkopf hollered back. "A graduate of Ronald McDonald Prep should know." As the rest of the crowd laughed, we Obnoxious Jerks waved our picket signs in the air and started our chant of "We want shorts!" again.

Alton turned away and caught up with Coach Arborio as he went back to his post as door monitor. Leslie followed to keep an eye on them while we continued our parade. By now it was almost as though we didn't remember we had the skirts on, except when one of us would take a little too long a stride and nearly go flying.

"I wonder what we're doing wrong," The Schneid said to Ippolito and me.

"What do you mean wrong?" Ippolito replied. "For once people actually seem to be supporting us."

"Yeah," The Schneid agreed. "That proves we must be doing something wrong."

Leslie came back and reminded us about a plan we'd discussed the night before. Then the five-minute warning bell sounded. The crowd broke up and started across the street, with us in the middle of it. We lowered our picket signs to avoid trouble as we approached the row of doors at the front of the school. We headed for the door farthest away from Arborio, and we tossed our picket signs in the trash cans right outside.

"Hey! I warned you!" he screamed at us as we washed inside with the human wave. "You can't come in here!"

We just ignored him and went right through the doors. He started toward us, but by then we'd split up and headed in different directions toward our various homerooms. Arborio made it into the hallway and kept shouting "Hey!" But he knew he had to make some kind of decision.

His decision was to head in the direction The Schneid and I were going. "Hey! You guys! In the skirts!"

We hurried away as fast as the skirts would let us, but we were no match for a jock in running shoes. Fortunately our homeroom was just down the hall.

We managed to get through the door just before Arborio did. The brain-alive among the class heard us skid in, looked at us, and cracked up as we headed for our seats.

"Mr. Schneider and Mr. Wess," said Mrs. Corrigan. "What do you think you're doing?"

"Taking our seats," I said.

"Dressed like that?" she inquired.

Arborio stormed through the door. "Come on, 'guys.' Let's go."

"What did they do?" Mrs. Corrigan asked.

"They know what they did." Arborio tapped his foot impatiently. "You can see most of it for yourself." He was one tough customer. Everybody else in the room was dripping, and he hadn't so much as broken a sweat.

"We didn't do anything," The Schneid insisted.

"You can see what they're wearing," Arborio went on. "They're not allowed in school dressed like this. Let's go, you two."

"We're not going anywhere," The Schneid said. "Check it out. We haven't done anything, and we're staying put."

Arborio gave us this exasperated look and pointed toward his feet. "Now," he said firmly.

"No," I answered just as firmly, and pointed my finger at him. "We're not moving. Everybody around here always talks about the rules. That's what we have rules for,' you keep hearing. Well, we're not breaking any of the rules. Look it up."

"I think I'll do just that," Mrs. Corrigan said.

"No need," said Arborio. "You guys are just making it worse for yourselves."

She made this little "just hold on a minute" gesture at him. Then she reached in her top desk drawer for a copy of the student handbook. "Schneider and Wess, sit down while we're sorting this out."

We sat down. But if my heart had been pounding before, it was pumping halfway out of my rib cage now. Arborio just stood there glaring at us with his arms folded across his chest. Mrs. Corrigan thumbed through the handbook and found the dress code. Then she walked over to Arborio and showed it to him. You could see all the muscles in his face slacken just for an instant. Then they tensed up again. "We'll just see about that," Arborio said, and went out the door. The late bell sounded.

"What are you guys trying to prove, anyway?" Mrs. Corrigan asked us.

"That we ought to be able to wear shorts on days like this," said The Schneid.

Applause and cries of "Right on!" came from the rest of the class.

"Good luck," said Mrs. Corrigan.

The P.A. came on with the usual boring morning announcements, plus a special message from Principal Helena Rojewski, who sympathized with everybody during the unexpected heat wave, but reminded everybody that UGMH had standards to maintain, and low-cut tops and short pants remained unacceptable. Everybody groaned and hooted.

Then old Crawley got on the P.A. and read in a dull monotone, "Will the following students please report to the vice-principal's office at once: Sims, Wilbert ('Strike one,' muttered The Schneid); Ippolito, Joseph; Garcia,

Robert ('Strike two,' I whispered); Daley, Michael; Wu, Perry; Schwarzkopf, Barry ('He's out!' cried The Schneid); Schneider, Dennis; and West, Frank."

Some of the class booed. "Strike four," I said out loud, tossing my bookpack on my shoulder and waiting till The Schneid had done the same thing.

"They don't have a leg to stand on," Mrs. Corrigan said encouragingly, smiling and waving the *Ullman Griswold Memorial High School Student Handbook* in the air.

"Not as long as it's covered down to the knee," I replied as we headed out the door.

24

"Here we go," said the Schneid.

Crawley was standing right inside the glass door of the administration office, staring impatiently into the hallway. The instant we came through the door, The Creepy One pointed sternly toward his office.

The Schneid and I stopped and breathed sighs of relief. The reason Crawley wasn't standing out in the hallway the way he usually did was that the administration office was air-conditioned to a perfectly comfortable temperature. The cool, dry air felt terrific. Behind the counter the secretaries looked up and giggled at us in our skirts.

Crawley pointed again. "Inside," he said sternly.

We went into his office and made ourselves comfortable. Our picket signs were leaning against the back wall behind Crawley's desk, but the rest of our crew hadn't showed up yet. "So cool in here!" The Schneid said, pulling the wet cloth of his shirt off his chest and flapping it around to help it dry out. "Demetrios doesn't know what he's missing."

Two more guys in skirts came through the door. "Hey," I said, "it's Barry and Robert!"

Garcia scowled. "You'd think Creepy could at least get half the names right, Mr. West."

"I'll bet Wilbert's real delighted too," Schwarzkopf said.

Sims sashayed in. "Hey, don't pick on old Crawley. He's improving. Last time it was Delbert."

"How'd your homeroom react?" Schwarzkopf wanted to know.

"Big laugh, a little applause, a lot of 'Go for it,'" Sims said. "One of the brain-dead girls asked me where I bought the sucker."

"It's incredible," Schwarzkopf said. "All the way over to Perry's house, all anybody could do was make snide remarks. Now that they know this is all a protest, it's mostly support. Even a couple of Lords came up and flashed thumbs-up."

"In my homeroom too," said Wu as he and Daley and Ippolito came through the door.

"Same here," Daley agreed. "Next thing you know, they'll be recruiting us for the football team."

"Or the cheerleading squad," Ippolito said.

"We'd need to shorten these a little," Schwarzkopf pointed out.

Crawley followed them in and shut the door. He shook his head. "Now, what I am going to do about this?"

"Hey, we're cool," Ippolito said. "These skirts are well within dress-code guidelines."

"Coach Arborio said you were protesting on school grounds," Crawley informed us.

"Coach Arborio is full of Chipiritos," said Schwarzkopf.

"Right," Perry Wu piped up. "We stayed across the

street the whole time. We threw out our picket signs as soon as we crossed over to school."

Crawley sighed and gave us a look of resignation.

"And the skirts are perfectly legal, according to the dress code," said Garcia, tossing a copy of the student handbook on Crawley's desk. "Read for yourself."

Crawley shook his head. "I know the code. I admit it."

"Coach Arborio doesn't," I said.

"He does now," Crawley replied.

"So what are we in here for, then?" Wu wondered.

"I'm just trying to figure out what's with you guys," Crawley said. "I mean, you all get good grades. What's your story? Why all this attitude?"

"Attitude in general, or attitude in particular?" Ippolito inquired.

"Either," said Crawley.

"The reason we're wearing skirts," The Schneid said patronizingly, as though he were talking to a very stupid first-grader, "is to protest the stupid dress code? The part about not being able to wear shorts?"

"Everybody hates it. It's stupid," Garcia added. "It's so hot you can barely think, and you have to worry about dying of heat prostration."

"I can't wear shorts either," said Crawley.

"Who says?" Daley asked.

Crawley hesitated. "Well, it wouldn't really be right if I did, would it?"

"Who says?" Daley repeated. "Is there a rule?"

"Not exactly," Crawley admitted.

"So it's your own free choice," Garcia said. "You could wear shorts if you wanted to."

Crawley sighed. "I could. But it wouldn't be professional."

"It would if you were a professional tennis player," said Daley.

"That's exactly it. Appropriateness. For me, shorts would be as inappropriate as a business suit on a tennis player."

"Besides, it'd be kind of overkill wearing shorts in here," said Sims. "You've got the air-conditioning blasting away so hard *I* feel like putting on a suit."

"Right," said Garcia. "I mean, have you ever sat in one of those classrooms on a day like today? It's like being a human french fry."

"What we really should wear out there is those outfits the bedouins wear in the desert," said The Schneid.

"Except they never heard of this kind of humidity," Planet Daley pointed out. "We'd stew in our own juices."

"What do you think we're doing now?" said three or four of us in unison.

Crawley made a little steeple with his hands and propped his chin on it. "All right. Go back to your classes."

"What about changing the rule about shorts?" said Daley.

"We'll take it under advisement," said Crawley.

"That means no way in hell," said Schwarzkopf.

"Watch your language," Crawley ordered. "I said we'll take it under advisement. Now go. Get back to your classes. Learn something."

"That's *it*?" said Schwarzkopf, amazed.

Crawley nodded.

"Mind if we stick around awhile until we cool off?" The Schneid asked.

"Go," Crawley said firmly.

We went.

"Something's wrong somewhere," The Schneid said as we headed back to our homeroom. "Crawley's got some kind of scheme brewing."

"That's what it seems like," I agreed. "But what?"

"I wish I knew," The Schneid said. "I wish I knew."

When we strolled back into our homeroom, the whole class applauded. "What did I tell you?" said Mrs. Corrigan.

Then the P.A. system blared out. "Your attention please. Your attention please. There will be an emergency meeting of the Student Council in the Council Room at ten o'clock this morning. All members are excused from class for the duration of the meeting. Repeating . . ."

"I knew it," The Schneid whispered.

"Knew what?" I whispered back.

"You just wait. By eleven o'clock this morning it'll be against the dress code for guys to wear skirts."

I looked at him in amazement. As soon as he finished saying it, I knew he had to be right.

"They call it democratic government," said The Schneid.

"So do the Russians," I replied.

25

When I first spotted her standing outside Mlle. Feldstein's room from way down the hall, Leslie was nervously biting her nails. When she spotted me coming down the hall in my skirt without a straitjacket on, she brightened up considerably.

"I can't believe Crawley let you go!" she exclaimed. "What happened?"

"You're right. You are not going to believe this," I said, and gave her the Ernest Hemingway version—the short short story, right down to the upraised fists of solidarity we both could see as we stood there in the corridor. Oh, there were a few upraised fingers, too, but that's almost like a standard brain-dead reflex when anything new or different comes along.

Then I told her what The Schneid said about the Student Council meeting. "No doubt about it," she said glumly. "That's exactly what those morons are going to do."

"Well, I can tell you one thing they are not going to do once they outlaw the skirts," said Wilver Sims.

"What's that?" Leslie asked.

"They are not going to let us walk around in our gym shorts all day."

"*Exactement,* as Mlle. Feldstein would say," I said.

"Merci," said Sims. "By the way, Les, is there anything you can do about this thing? It was okay before, but now it's pinching like a crab."

Leslie tugged at the waist of Sims's skirt. "Feels okay. It fit this morning, didn't it?"

"Yeah, but it sure hurts now," Wilver said in a strange tone. "Take a closer look."

Leslie suspected something. "Oh, no. You've probably got something awful planned." She took a step back.

"Come on," Wilver said sincerely. "This thing is driving me crazy."

Leslie moved in for a closer inspection. "I'm telling you, Wilver—*AAAAaaaaah!!!!*"

Leslie jumped back ten feet. Somehow Wilver had rigged up a giant cloth snake to shoot out at her from underneath the skirt.

"I knew it, damn you! I knew it!" Leslie shrieked. "You've got a sick mind, Wilver Sims!" And then she cracked up. So did I.

"Told you it was pinching," Sims said without cracking a smile. Then Garcia showed up, and we all went inside together. Safety in numbers.

"Ah, très, très beau," said Mlle. Feldstein when she saw us three semitransvestites walk in. *"Nous avon aujourd'hui une leçon de genre,"* meaning today we were studying gender. She actually made some pretty fair jokes about it in French. Once you got *jupe*—the word for "skirt"—the rest was easy.

In between first and second period a junior guy named Clark something (it wasn't Kent) and a senior girl named Winona Warren from *The Griswold Gazette* came up to interview us and take our pictures. I don't exactly know how they found us, but the guy snapped the picture first thing and disappeared. Winona stuck with me to my next class, interviewing all the way.

"Can I quote you on that as the spokesman for the Obnoxious Jerks?" she kept asking every time I answered one of her questions. I had to keep explaining that I wasn't a spokesman for anybody, but that I personally believed the shorts rule was totally ridiculous and so did all the other members and every other sane person at Griswold High. The last thing I needed was for the guys to get the crazy idea that I was claiming to be a spokesman for us. The whole idea of an official spokesman wasn't something the Obnoxious Jerks would approve of.

When I got to the cafeteria for lunch, a whole bunch of people were already hanging around our table asking questions about our protest, lending support, or telling us what dorks we were. Ippolito and a couple of the others were actually setting up dates with some gorgeous airhead girls who wouldn't have come within fifty feet of them the day before.

I also found out that Winona and Clark had gotten around. A couple of the other guys had been interviewed, and most of us had had our pictures taken.

"Hey, that's great," I said. "One way or another we ought to make Friday's *Gazette*."

"Probably another," said Ippolito glumly.

"You haven't been around long enough to get it, Back," said Daley. "The *Gazette* is a total puppet of the administration."

"Yeah," said Demetrios. "Planet and I both quit last year when they killed one of his stories about how lousy the soccer team was."

"I can see the caption on our pictures now," Daley said. *"Skirts: Protest or Prank?"*

"Prank," said Leslie Freeze, stopping at our table. "Definitely a prank."

She just stood there while everybody decided what to do. Our table was unofficially reserved for members of the Obnoxious Jerks, and she was almost an honorary member. Still, none of us wanted to be the first to invite her to join us. I didn't know why, after all Leslie had done. Old customs die hard, I guess; I didn't say anything either.

"Will somebody invite me to sit down?" she finally asked.

"Sit down," most of us said at the same time, and she did, about as far as she could get from me. I wasn't sure if she was making a point or not.

"Anybody hear anything about that Student Council meeting?" she asked.

"We were looking around before," The Schneid told her. "There's nobody in here who's on the council. That means the meeting hasn't broken up yet."

"Or something," said Schwarzkopf. "Maybe they decided to spend our student funds on a fancy restaurant."

"Wouldn't be the first time," Daley muttered with his mouth full.

And that's when we heard those dreaded words from the P. A. system: "Your attention please."

"Here come our student representatives," mumbled Ippolito, pointing his thumb toward the door. Members of the council began to file in.

"Here comes our doom, you mean," said Sims.

"Your attention please," the P. A. system repeated. A few of us stood up and saluted. Then we sat down again.

There were a couple more "Attention please" 's, followed by a long pause. Finally Vice-Principal Crawley's voice announced, "At the suggestion of the administration, the Student Council met this morning in an emergency session. The result is a modification to the student code."

"Here it comes," Perry Wu said.

"Paragraph ten, section c, will now read: 'Skirts must be long enough to reach the top of the knee. Blue denim skirts will not be permitted. Male students are not permitted to wear dresses, skirts, or other feminine attire.'"

There was a lot of booing in the cafeteria. We Obnoxious Jerks simply nodded at each other and shook our heads. We'd already guessed. There was nothing to say.

"Section d will also be modified. It will now read: 'Short pants will not be permitted—'"

There was a loud groan before Crawley continued.

"'—except on days when the National Weather Service forecasts maximum temperatures of eighty degrees Fahrenheit or more.'"

There was a brief, stunned silence. All of a sudden the whole lunchroom let out an enormous roar. Just as suddenly, Wilver Sims climbed up on our table and began a sort of victory dance with little bows in every direction. Daley followed him, and the rest of us joined in. Sims grabbed Leslie's arm and pulled her up to share our triumph. Everybody in the cafeteria was looking at us as the P. A. system blared on over the commotion.

"I would like to make it clear that this was a decision of your administration, working with the Student Council members who brought the situation to our attention," Crawley said.

"Remember, it had nothing to do with us!" Schwarzkopf shouted at the top of his lungs. The non-brain-dead half of the cafeteria laughed and applauded.

"Get down off of there!" came rasping through the

laughter. From our perch atop the table I could see Coach Arborio halfway across the cafeteria, striding angrily toward us.

"I think it's a tribute to the fine student members of the council," Crawley's voice added, "working cooperatively to correct a situation that became unpleasant during this unprecedented heat wave."

"Thank you, thank you, great gods of Student Council!" Schwarzkopf hooted. Most of the cafeteria laughed back and started applauding us. Daley and Sims and The Schneid hooked arms into a little chorus line and did a couple of high kicks—well, all right, low kicks—but then the tables started wobbling kind of scarily, so they stopped and gave each other high fives. We all started giving each other high fives. Demetrios even climbed up and joined in. It was great. It was the high point of the school year.

Then Arborio showed up. "Get down!" he snapped. "Now!"

"Get down and boogie?" Garcia asked.

"You know what I'm talking about. There's no standing on the cafeteria tables. Period."

"What are you worried about?" The Schneid said. "You'd probably be glad if one fell down and we broke our heads or something."

"Off. Now." He slammed his hand down on the table to make the point.

"Fun while it lasted," said The Schneid. Sims and the rest of us kind of waved good-bye to the crowd. Some of the kids around the room waved back. Others applauded or booed. This time we were positive the boos were for Arborio.

"Crawley's office," Coach said. "You guys know where it is. You too, miss."

Leslie smiled at him. "It's an honor and a privilege."

And it was. Crawley was feeling pretty proud of

himself. He confiscated our skirts—not Leslie's of course—and made us walk around in our gym shorts all day.

But that was fine, because normally wearing gym shorts to class wasn't permitted. Our gym shorts let people know who the real heroes of the Great Shorts Protest were. And a lot of people who otherwise wouldn't have given us the time of day came up to congratulate us.

The only bad part was having to serve two hours of detention. *"Ex post facto!"* Daley protested. "Constitutionally illegal!"

Crawley was prepared for that line of argument. He insisted the detention didn't have anything to do with the new dress-code rules. Our punishment was strictly for violating the rule about standing on the cafeteria tables.

But who cared? We had won! Old Man Nilon was running detention that afternoon. Even he congratulated us.

26

Detention didn't dampen our spirits one bit. We felt incredible. We had won! We all left school hollering and laughing together, the full complement of Obnoxious Jerks, including our brand-new honorary-member-to-be. The greatest jerk-out of all time had been successful beyond our wildest dreams. We were hot stuff, and it wasn't just the temperature. We must have burned up the phone wires that night talking about it, replaying it with each other. Leslie and I alone must have spent close to an hour going over all the crazy things that had happened in the various classrooms.

The next day there must have been only half a dozen kids in the entire school who weren't wearing shorts. We heard there was a little flurry of stupidity from a couple of the brain-dead teachers about the fact that most of the girls' shorts did not come down to their kneecaps, but the new dress code didn't say anything about that, and the administration probably figured it was a good idea to leave well enough alone for a while. As for us, we were still sort of celebrities. People kept coming up and congratulating us. Except for Student Council members like Lord George Alton. Alton went out of his way to tell us what creeps we were and insist that the Student Council's efforts were the only reason anybody was wearing shorts today. We just laughed at him. What else can you do with somebody like that?

That night there was a terrific thunderstorm that actually knocked the power out for half an hour. Wednesday morning it was chilly enough that nobody was wearing shorts anywhere. On Thursday Crawley actually gave us back our skirts.

And when we got to school Friday morning, *The Griswold Gazette* was piled up in the usual stacks just inside the doors. Ippolito and I stopped and took a couple. The headline was **Council, Administration Change Shorts Code.** There was a picture that had to have been from Tuesday, full of kids wearing shorts and grinning at the camera. And the story was a masterpiece:

> In the face of a record heat wave, the Administration and Student Council agreed Monday to modify the portion of the dress code prohibiting shorts. "The rule had outworn its usefulness," stated Vice-Principal Alexander Crawley. "And we were happy to work with the Student Council to change it."

"Give me a break!" I groaned.

> Student Council President Gail Johansen agreed. "We've never had a problem with this rule before. But the brutal heat wave of the past two weeks made wearing shorts important

to many of our students, particularly the boys. We're glad that the Council and the Administration could work together in the best spirit of cooperation."

"Which you will definitely need, Gail, if you hope to get a good college recommendation," Ippolito said.

Students were delighted at the action. Freshman John Tallmadge said, "It's a relief to be able to get a little cooler." Senior Malrena Carlan agreed: "We've never had a heat wave like this that I can remember during the school year. Wearing shorts is really nice in this kind of weather."

"This week's heat was really demoralizing. Changing the code was an important step forward, and we Council members worked hard for it," said sophomore George Alton.

"Oh, make me puke." I stuck my finger in my throat.

The changed rule for shorts may not make much difference for the rest of the school year. Tuesday's thunderstorm spelled the end of the heat wave and brought mild temperatures to the Froston area once again. No high temperatures are predicted for the coming week.

One other minor change was made to the same paragraph of the dress code.

"One minor change!" I shouted. "There's not a word about us!"

"Not even a word about skirts," Ippolito said. "That's why Demetrios and Daley quit the *Gazette*. Hey, they never mentioned our talent show act either, remember."

I remembered all right. "Or Leslie's."

"And look at the dumb caption under the picture," Ippolito went on. " 'Shorts were the fashion statement of the day Tuesday on legs throughout Griswold High.' "You know why this is?" Ippolito waved the paper angrily in the air.

I shrugged.

"The administration doesn't want trouble," Ippolito went on. "If they let the paper report what really happened, the school board might not think everything's just fine here. So it's all news is good news."

When I ran into Leslie outside Mlle. Feldstein's class, she couldn't believe it either. "Did you see this piece of kitty litter?"

I just nodded.

"We did everything, and they didn't even mention us. Not once!"

I nodded again.

"Doesn't it make you angry?"

"It did," I said. "It's just part of the way things are around here."

"Hey, calm down, Les," said Wilver Sims.

"Why?" Leslie demanded.

"You should understand by now. That kind of thing is typical. Happens all the time. It's why we do jerk-outs."

"Huh?" Leslie said.

"Keeps the world off balance," I replied. "They can't just get away with it and pretend nobody notices."

"Right," said Sims. "It keeps things real. Keeps us real too."

And he was right. With the cool weather and the end of the shorts thing, we were already nobodies again. Everybody was treating us exactly the same way they had treated us before. Nothing had changed. The girls who had wanted to go out with some of us all canceled their dates. Daley pointed out that if you asked twenty kids how shorts suddenly became legal according to the dress code, maybe two would remember the protest and what really happened. It was true. It was sad.

That afternoon, before the Obnoxious Jerks meeting at The Schneid's, I noticed Ippolito and Leslie standing away from everybody else at the far end of the dining room. They were making these big gestures as though they were yelling at each other, but they kept their voices down so you couldn't hear what they were saying.

"Do any of you guys know what the deal is between those two?" I asked.

"Sixth grade," Schwarzkopf mumbled through a mouthful of Chipiritos.

"What about sixth grade?" I pressed.

Schwarzkopf shrugged and stuffed more Chipiritos into his mouth. I glanced around the room inquisitively.

"Hey, don't look at us," said The Schneid. "Harry's the only one who went to that elementary school."

I stared at Schwarzkopf again. "I heard the story secondhand," he muttered. "I was out sick when it happened."

"When what happened?" I demanded.

Schwarzkopf swallowed. "The way I heard it, it had something to do with this class project where the teacher paired us up boy-girl to do research on marriage and stuff. The teacher teamed Leslie with Joe." He stuffed his mouth again.

"And?" I pressed.

"Why is this so important to you, Back?" Garcia asked.

"I'm curious, okay? Come on, Harry. That can't be all of it."

"I told you, I wasn't there. Supposedly she said something like, 'God, not Nipple-ito!' to some friend of hers a little too loud so the rest of the class heard it. Joe had to carry that nickname around for the rest of the year. I mean, he already had it—it was kind of unavoid-

205

able—but now that it was out in the open, even girls weren't afraid to use it to his face."

Schwarzkopf reached toward the bowl of Chipiritos between it. I snatched it out of his grasp.

"That's half of it. Fine. But why's she mad at him?"

"Joe got back at her somehow," Schwarzkopf said. "The way I heard it, he set up some kind of trap to stare at her naked in the girls' locker room. Not just him, but a bunch of his friends too. Now will you pass me those Chipiritos, please?"

I held the bowl away from him. "You sure about all this? Sounds really scuzzy."

"It was damned scuzzy. If it was true. But then he hung out with a bunch of *real* jerks back then. They used to make snide remarks at me on the way home from school. Most of them are Lords or Viscounts now. Give me those Chipiritos, or there is going to be trouble."

As I handed the bowl back to him, I felt kind of weird and sad. In a way I almost wished I hadn't brought all this stuff out in the open. True, I knew a little more than I did before. But I didn't even know if I really knew what I thought I knew. Schwarzkopf didn't have the whole story, and the part he thought he had might not even have been true. Joe and Leslie were probably smart to have kept it between themselves all this time. They were right: It really wasn't any of my business.

They came back in from the dining room.

"What was that all about?" The Schneid inquired.

Ippolito shrugged. "Personal stuff."

"Meaning what?" I asked in spite of myself.

"Meaning personal stuff. Okay?" He gave me this look that said he wasn't going to discuss it.

Leslie was standing by the dining room. I went over to her. "Everything okay?" I asked.

Leslie shrugged.

"He's not still giving you a hard time?" I pressed.

"Everything's cool," she said.

"Are you friends now?"

"I wouldn't put it just that way," she said. "Let it go, okay?"

Schwarzkopf handed her a bowlful of Official Tortilla Chips, but Leslie passed—too salty, she said. Then The Schneid pounded his Doola Cola can on the table. We sang our national anthem. We waived the reading of the minutes. We heard the report from our temporary treasurer.

"Old business?" The Schneid asked.

Schwarzkopf stood up. "We're on a roll," he said formally, and put on his glasses.

"Uh-oh," said Daley.

"I would like to read a letter we received. This is from the Chipiritos division of the Amerimex National Bakery Corporation."

"You mean somebody actually answered one of your letters?" Demetrios laughed.

"Silence," said Schwarzkopf with a majestic sweep of his hand. "This was sent to 'Harry Schwarzkopf, Ad Hoc Endorsement Chairman, The Obnoxious Jerks,' my home address. 'Dear Mr. Schwarzkopf,' it reads. 'Thank you for informing us about the endorsement of our Jalapeño Flavor Chipiritos as the Official Tortilla Chip of the Obnoxious Jerks. This is indeed an honor we are proud to receive.'"

"About as proud as receiving the plague," Daley muttered.

Schwarzkopf shot him a dirty look over his glasses. He went on: "'We value your interest in Chipiritos and are delighted to know you enjoy them so much you would appreciate free samples. However—'"

"Here it comes," Ippolito interrupted.

"'However,'" Schwarzkopf repeated, "'we would prefer to honor your request by making the Obnoxious

Jerks full-fledged members of The International Chipiritos Club. Simply send five dollars and seventy-five cents for each of your members, along with your shirt size, and we will return one T-Shirt for each member, along with an official membership card conveying all rights and appurtenances. Thank you for honoring us with your endorsement; you may be sure it has been received with all the appreciation it deserves.' "

"Like none," said The Schneid. Schwarzkopf gave him a dirty look. "Oops. Sorry. The chair disciplines himself." The Schneid pounded the can of Doola Cola on his head and called for order.

" 'Sincerely yours,' " Schwarzkopf went on, " 'A. Meyer Tonkin, President, Chipirito and Snack Food Division, Amerimex National Bakery Corporation.' "

"Gee," said Garcia. "How nice of them."

"It brings a warm glow to my heart," said Wu.

"And kind of a hot belching sensation to my stomach," said Ippolito.

"Don't worry, guys," said Schwarzkopf. "Our endorsement is an honor we don't grant lightly. I'm confident Doola Cola will come across with some freebies."

"Five-dollar-and-seventy-five-cent freebies," Perry Wu snorted.

Schwarzkopf took off his glasses and sat down.

"Any more old business?" asked The Schneid. There wasn't any. "New business?"

I started to jump to my feet, but Schwarzkopf beat me to it. "I have some nominations for new Official Products. Rose-bol: the Official Toilet Bowl Cleaner of the Obnoxious Jerks."

"Harry, will you give us a break?" Garcia broke in. "Just once?"

"We're already running late," Demetrios said. "And we missed softball last week on account of the heat."

Schwarzkopf sat down and scowled. "Just wait till next week."

"Thank you," said The Schneid.

Schwarzkopf harrumphed and sulked.

"More new business?" The Schneid inquired.

I stood up. "We have an honorary member to induct. I believe you all know Leslie Freeze."

She bowed a little without standing up.

"Do I hear a motion to add Leslie Freeze as an honorary member of the Obnoxious Jerks?" asked The Schneid.

"Why not?" said Roberto Garcia.

"Do I hear a second?"

"Second!" squawked Harry Schwarzkopf.

"Moved and seconded," said The Schneid. "All—"

"Wait a second," Wilver Sims interrupted.

"Wait a second?" replied The Schneid.

"Yeah," said Sims. "Let's forget this 'honorary' nonsense. Let's make her a real member and get it over with once and for all."

Leslie gave him an enormous smile.

"Is that an amendment to Wess's motion?" The Schneid asked.

"Yeah," said Sims.

"Fine with me," I said.

"Seconded," said Schwarzkopf.

"All right, then," said The Schneid. "The motion on the floor is to make Leslie Freeze a full-fledged member of the Obnoxious Jerks. All in favor, please trumpet like a wounded elephant."

There was a whole lot of trumpeting going on. But above it all you could hear Ippolito shouting, "Wait a second! Wait a second!"

The commotion died down. "The chair recognizes Joe Ippolito."

"I would like a roll-call vote, please," Ippolito said.

I could see Leslie suddenly tense up. I wondered what Ippolito was up to. Was he trying to go back on our promise or make sure her membership was only honorary or embarrass her again or what?

"A roll-call vote?" Garcia said. "We've never had a roll-call vote before."

"There's always a first time," Ippolito said.

"Let's get it over with," said Daley.

"Do I have to figure out alphabetical order?" said The Schneid.

"Just going around the room is fine," Daley claimed.

"All right," said The Schneid. "Wu?"

Wu trumpeted like a wounded elephant.

"A simple yes or no, please," said The Schneid. "I assume that was a yes?"

"Right," said Wu.

The Schneid pointed to Garcia.

"Aye."

"Yup," said Sims.

"All right," said Demetrios.

"Yessiree Bob," said Schwarzkopf.

"Okeydokey," said Daley.

"Yea," I said.

It was Ippolito's turn, but he didn't answer right away. He looked at me. He looked at Leslie. He looked at the rest of us. Then he said, "Yes, indeed."

"Show-off," muttered Schwarzkopf.

"I make it unanimous," said The Schneid. "Okay: I now pronounce you, Leslie Freeze, a full-fledged, one-hundred-percent Obnoxious Jerk! All please rise for the Obnoxious Jerk salute!"

Everybody stuffed his mouth with Jalapeño Flavor Chipiritos and crunched as loud as he could. On cue from The Schneid everybody shouted "Caramba!" Chipiritos went flying everywhere. I wondered if for a moment Leslie almost felt a rush of power not lightly given to mortal men—or women.

"I will never forget this ceremony as long as I live,"

she said with all the phoniness of an actress accepting an Oscar. "It is an honor I will cherish the rest of my life."

Then she cracked us up with an imitation of Old Man Nilon saying "You know, you guys really are obnoxious jerks." She'd actually been in that class on the historic day our club received its name. In a way she'd been one of us since the beginning.

Jalapeño Flavor Chipirito crumbs can really sting your eyes. A tear ran down Leslie's cheek. Five different members rushed to her rescue with tissues.

Ippolito looked at me. I looked at him. He'd been right the first time: The Obnoxious Jerks would never be the same.

"Hey! More new business!" Leslie shouted once the tear was taken care of. "I've got this great idea for the next jerk-out. . . ."

No doubt about it. We'd never be the same. But there was a pretty fair chance that we might just be better than ever. And in a way I was the one who was sort of responsible. I knew I'd never get credit for it unless Leslie turned out to be a real drip, but I felt pretty good about it all the same.

That was the moment when a fact of major significance suddenly chose to pop into my head. "Petie!" I burst out, pointing at Leslie.

"Hey, right!" she exclaimed, flashing her million-dollar smile at me personally, which I didn't exactly mind.

Schwarzkopf scowled. "Petie?"

"The Little Rascals' dog!" Leslie explained.

"What does the Little Rascals' dog have to do with the Obnoxious Jerks?" Ippolito demanded.

Leslie and I just shrugged and kept it to ourselves. Face it: There are some things that just aren't anybody else's business.

But then I also had to face the fact that another one of my brilliant ideas might not be so brilliant after all. As I looked around the room, I suddenly realized that now there were at least seven other guys who wanted to be Leslie Freeze's favorite Obnoxious Jerk.

At least I had a head start.

ABOUT THE AUTHOR

STEPHEN MANES is a versatile and popular author, journalist, and screenwriter. He is a contributing editor and regular columnist for *PC Magazine,* and his work has been the subject of several public television programs. Stephen Manes has published more than twenty books, including *Video War, I'll Live, Chicken Trek, The Boy Who Turned Into a TV Set, Be a Perfect Person in Just Three Days!,* and *It's New! It's Improved! It's Terrible!*